Dragon Tender

Book Three of the Fae Unbound Series

Jill Nojack

IndieHeart Press

Kent, Ohio

Cover designed by Lou Harper.

Visit the series website for series related content:

www.faeunbound.com

Dragon Tender / Jill Nojack. — 1st ed.

ISBN: 978-0-9911234-6-9

CHAPTER ONE

My Own Face Inside The Trees

AVENALL LEANED BACK AGAINST the trunk of the tree, his natural grace helping him balance easily on the wide branch. He'd received a new flash drive full of music from his human friend Danton today, and he closed his eyes, leaning his head back to relax as he pressed earbuds into his ears. Danton called this music "prog rock". Human music was so different from the slow, passionless chanting of the elves. Every time Danton gave him more, the different feel of each new style swept him away.

Minutes into the second song, he startled from his trance when the branches of the tree reached out to twine around him. His mouth opened in a gasp, but a branch snaked around his head, gagging him so that he couldn't make a sound. As the tree's rough arms continued to twist and grow, eventually enclosing his body completely, he wondered if he'd somehow offended the spirits of the trees.

Would his life end here as he slowly starved to death in a wooden cage?

Then, in the gaps between the twigs and leaves that covered his face, he caught a glimpse of something that frightened him more than thoughts of slow starvation: his father came stamping through the forest toward the tree where he was hiding. He glanced overhead from time to time as he walked and then passed beyond the tree where Avenall was hidden. He heard the footsteps continue farther into the woods and held his breath until he was sure his father was gone.

Shortly after the rustling sound of footfalls faded, the branches began to loosen, treating him gently now. He looked around for the maker of his cocoon. On the large branch slightly above him, Oriane's head separated from the trunk of the tree. Bark transformed to flesh as she returned to her ambulatory shape. He turned away when a bare shoulder materialized and he realized she would not be dressed when she appeared.

After a few moments, he heard her soft voice. "I'm sorry, but I didn't have time to warn you. You can turn now. I'm robed."

Avenall turned back to her, smiling. Her blue gown set off the icy blue of her eyes and flowed softly over the many contours of her body. "My thanks to you. For a time, I thought I'd offended the dryads. I'm glad it was only you."

"It is best to keep in mind what could happen if you did offend us." She was smiling. He knew she loved to tease him. But to her, he was just a boy. No matter how much of his heart he held out to her, there was no hope she'd notice him in the way he wished. Even to his own people, he was a child. The elves would not consider him anything else until he'd attained an age of at least thirty years, and he had lived only seventeen. Oriane, who had been full grown in the time before the shadow realm, could not possibly view him as a man. Yet still, he hoped, and he sometimes convinced himself for a while that she shared his feelings.

"Do you want to hear the song? It's so free..."

"No, I do not want to hear! If your father discovers you sneaking away to listen to human music and watch those moving paintings on your machine, he would gladly swing the sword at your beheading. How can you be so foolish? You were nearly discovered."

Avenall shrugged. "Maybe it would be better for everyone if he did find out. He's made it clear since my magic bloomed that I will always be a disappointment to him. I had no control over the nature of the magic I was born with! At least I can tend the dragons with it. I might have had so little magic that I could only tend the cows, the pigs, and the chickens, and be valued by my people only slightly more than humans are."

"There is nothing wrong with the magic you have. Your gift to share the mind of the creatures around us is a blessing. If the elves weren't so arrogant, they would hold you in esteem for your gift—to ride in the minds of dragons—how can they not see the beauty in that?"

Avenall dropped the stick he'd been using to tap out a beat against his hand and watched it fall to the forest floor. "It's hard to believe in my value when everyone but you says I have so little. But even so, I love tending the dragons. I love sharing their minds. I wouldn't have a warrior's magic even if it was possible." He aggressively shoved a loose strand of long blonde hair back from where it crept over one green eye. "I would live among the humans if I could. With them, I could be whatever I want to be."

"Yes. As long as that did not include being an elf. Not all humans are accepting of fae."

"No, but I could go to the Queen. Look..." Avenall queued up one of the videos Danton had brought him and held it out to Oriane so she could watch. "Do you see? The Queen wants us all to live together as friends. Like Danton and I are friends, like your sister Euphemia is friends with the Queen and her mother."

"Yes, but she is not the same queen who led us in the shadow realm. Morgan is gone. While I support this young queen, she has not united the fae as Morgan did. Your people show her little respect. I think because she associates herself with the Abomination."

"She says this Thomas isn't Faolan since she removed his memories. She is the queen—I will believe her."

"Avie, I think you only like her because she is human. I fear you long to be human as well."

Another elf would have struck her brutally at the suggestion. Avenall only turned his face to the ground and shook his head sadly. Then he returned his gaze to hers and sighed. "No. I just want to be me. And me? I like human music. And I like humans, even though I am elf.

CHAPTER TWO
The Magic Store

THOMAS GROUND THE SEEDS fine, then measured the resulting powder carefully into small plastic pouches. Focused on his task, he didn't hear Tanji sneak up behind him and didn't feel her magic there, either. He startled a little when her arms slipped around his waist and she whispered in his ear, "If you don't start paying attention when someone comes into the shop, I'm going to have to let you go—from the job, I mean. I'm not feeling like letting you go physically right at the moment." She stood on her tiptoes and punctuated her sentence with a playful kiss on the back of his neck. "But I also don't want shoplifters making off with all of the goods because you're not paying attention."

He looked up and saw that a customer had come into the shop while he was working, just as she'd said. He had no idea how long the teen had been there, and she certainly looked like she was looking for something to steal: she was hyper-alert, and he could feel the mild crackle of pixie magic coursing through her system. Definitely a duster. But his mind had been on other things. Important things. Not foolish things like whether or not some chav made off with a pocketful of crystals.

He didn't respond to Tanji's teasing. "I was woolgathering. Sorry." He began carefully labeling and pricing the packets. She stepped away from him and walked to his side, where she turned and, in a swift and graceful movement, hopped up to sit on the wooden counter.

"I'd say you aren't any fun anymore, but that would assume that you were bunches of fun at some other point. And since we both know that's not true, is there a reason why you're being even more serious than usual?"

He didn't look at her, instead splitting his focus between the packets and the duster girl as she moved around the shop. It wasn't time for Tanji to know yet, but he was sure she'd approve when he told her. He shook his head. "No, nothing different than usual. I just didn't hear her come in."

The girl looked over her shoulder and saw him looking directly at her as she lingered around the smaller items that would easily disappear into a pocket. She reconsidered when she saw his expression and made it easier on him by leaving. The bell on the door chimed softly as she exited.

"Look, Tom, if there's something we should talk about..."

"It isn't about us. It's not about you. I have other things I think about. I'm grateful to you and your father for letting me work in the shop, but you know I don't have a talent for retail. I have other plans, and sometimes I get caught up thinking about them."

"Such as?"

"I told you I have something I'm working on." He

smiled. "You'll be well chuffed when I can finally tell you about it, and you'll fancy me even more then."

Tanji fluttered long lashes above huge brown eyes. "Really? And what makes you think I fancy you now?"

She leaned forward, moving closer across the countertop, and he knew she hoped to collect a kiss. He often found her predictable. But she was beautiful, intelligent, and she was elven half-fae. He picked up the tray he'd just filled and started to the storeroom. "Sorry, guv. No time for games. The boss is a real slave driver."

He heard her sigh dramatically as he flicked the light switch in the storeroom and started rearranging a shelf to make room.

Thomas walked Tanji to her car that night with the snow falling lightly around them. Although he held her hand the whole time to show he could be attentive, he found it impossible to keep his mind on what she talked about. She had too many silly concerns.

Why would he care if dusting was a problem in her insignificant city? It was a waste of energy to worry about human children who used pixie dust to get high. He would soon be able to take her to one of the forest compounds in Europe where they could live among the elves and be a part of something so much greater than they were among the humans. All he had to do was keep his part of the deal, and he would be welcomed as the elves had promised. And why wouldn't he keep it gladly? He wanted the fae to have real power in the world again as much as the elves did.

He gave her a peck goodnight as she pulled him into her by the open flaps of his coat. She slipped her hands inside the flaps to warm them against his body; he could tell she wanted to linger. Being close to her like this made him want a longer goodbye too. But he had to go: he felt the vague stir of a wisp's magic somewhere down the street—maybe by the pond on the edge of the park? He had to go before it moved on. There were fewer wisps to be found in the city every day. Soon, there would be none.

He hurried down the street after pulling away, following the signal set for him by the wisp's magic. The sense of it got stronger as he moved closer, and his eagerness grew. His body tensed, anticipating the ritual.

The wisp hung like mist above the deep water in the center of the small pond. It was dark. No one would see. Thomas removed his clothes down to his shorts, folding them neatly and arranging them carefully in a tidy pile on the snow-dusted ground. Then he walked silently into the freezing water. If he had not been focused on his reward, his teeth would have chattered painfully. He was nearly chest deep by the time he was close enough to the wisp to influence it.

He opened his hands toward the wisp, his palms out and glowing now in pale blue. The wisp moved closer, then closer still. Thomas's palms blazed suddenly with bright magic as he closed his eyes, focused, and the wisp spread across his arms and chest before it melted into his body, leaving him breathing heavily and glowing with inner warmth in the sudden blackness.

Thomas smiled.

~~*

When Tanji opened the front door, she stepped back involuntarily: both of her parents were standing there waiting on her. Neither of them spoke. And what was la madre doing here? She wasn't due back from New York until next weekend.

After a moment of them all silently staring at each other, still standing in the doorway, Tanji said, "So...mom...dad... what's up?"

Her mother went first. "We want to talk to you, Toonkins. It's important. But we don't know how to start."

Tanji looked at her father, whose expression was unchar- acteristically serious. She said, "So. Maybe I could come in and sit down, then?"

Her parents looked at each other and smiled sad smiles, then they started toward the living room. Her father sat on one end of the couch. Her mother took the other. That didn't look right to her. She took the big chair across the coffee table from them so she could get to the door fast if bullets started flying.

Once she was seated, her mother spoke up in what was left of a musical Jamaican accent. "Well, I might as well say it, Tanji-girl. I've taken an apartment in New York, and I'll be living there full time from now on. I won't be coming home on the weekends anymore."

"But your job in New York was supposed to be tempo- rary! You were supposed to be coming home next month."

"I got a very good offer to stay." Her mother took a deep breath and looked away. When she looked back, tears wet the corners of her eyes. "And I want to be there. I never meant to hurt either of you. But I'm staying in New York. I'm sorry. I love this job. I love New York. It's everything I ever wanted for my career."

Tanji looked to her father, not knowing how to react. "Dad?"

"We've both tried to keep things going for your sake, but we've known for a good amount of time that we weren't going to be together once you left for college. Your mother and I want different things. We didn't think we'd divorce yet for a few years, but things change."

"But I'll stay here, right? I don't have to go to New York?" Tanji looked back to her mother.

"No, you don't have to go to New York. My taking you away—that would be the thing that would break your father's heart. I would never do that."

"But I get to come visit, right?"

Her mother moved around the coffee table and hugged her, "Whenever you want. I'll be in town for the next two weeks to tie up loose ends, and I'll see you as often as I can before I leave. We'll have a least one nice long mother and daughter dinner, and we'll talk."

Tanji shrugged her mother off and stood up. "Okay, so I'm sending myself to my room now. I don't know what to think about this." But she did know that she wanted to talk to her best friend. There was no point in calling her boyfriend. He'd react to the news like a block of wood. *What good is he to me anyway, if I know he won't even be there for me when I'm sad?*

She realized in that moment that there was going to be another breakup in the family soon. She grabbed her phone and flicked the contact for Lizbet, hoping her BFF picked up before she started crying.

CHAPTER THREE

Can't Get You Out of My Head

AVENALL ATE HIS MEAGER breakfast of bread and cheese alone in his sleeping loft, then went outside to the rain barrel and washed his hands and face. He fed the dragons and made sure there was plenty of clean water available in their troughs.

When his morning routine was complete, he entered Mer's stall and approached the young dragon carefully, sending soothing thoughts and keeping his mind open to the thoughts of the dragon. Mer had been keeping himself contained and off from the others for a few days, and it was worrying. Mer usually enjoyed being near the larger dragons. He probed deeper into Mer's mind for any clue to what could be troubling him and found his answer in a bright flash of pain located along his hindquarters.

He extended his hand and laid it gently on the dragon's flanks, admiring as always the iridescent blue shine of Mer's scales. He ran his hand downward toward the source of the pain and felt the sharp splinter of wood jutting from the dragon's hide. He concentrated on reassuring the dragon as he pinched the small nub of the splinter that showed itself from beneath a scale, grasping it as firmly as he could and then easing it out of its hiding place.

He knew the dragon had turned at the tug and hoped he understood the message Avenall continued to send of helping, healing, and concern. If not, he might meet the same fate as many dragon tenders before him—burned to death by his own charges. When Mer realized the source of the pain had been removed, Avenall could feel him relax. His big head brushed affectionately against Avenall's shoulder by way of thanks, much as a cat would rub her cheek against the hand of the one who strokes her. Avenall relaxed, too. No fiery death today. And he could feel in the dragon's mind that his care had served to deepen their bond.

Avenall had only been the compound's dragon tender for a few months. Before that, he was an apprentice, learning the ways of the dragon tender but never in charge. The dragons had only begun to stop resisting him when he entered their minds. He knew from what he felt there that they missed Durian, their tender before him. Avenall missed him, too. He missed him deeply.

As he went to the bench at the side of the stable to find salve, he heard his father's voice just outside the stable door. He stood there silently, listening.

"It's distasteful, having to come down here to the stables knowing I will find my own son engaged as a stable hand. If I had any other children, I would disown him."

Avenall's heart, never cheered when his father was around, squeezed painfully at his father's words. He wanted to stop listening, but he couldn't tear himself away.

"He is at least a fine dragon tender, Elder Shan. All of the dragon riders say so. He has a way of keeping the dragons calmer than any of those before him."

"Faugh," he heard his father reply, followed by the sound of him hocking up spit and ridding himself of it noisily to emphasize his point. "He is still a dragon tender, nonetheless. A menial. I doubt he is even my child. If his mother had not abandoned him in her shame, she would have been made to confess her infidelity."

"Still, he will be useful when the dragon riders take to the sky again against the humans."

"As you say. But it does not make me proud to be burdened with a dragon tender for a son. And his time of usefulness may be sooner than you think, my friend. Your riders will bring us glory against the humans when they can no longer use any of their weapons or their technology. The battle will favor us again." Avenall strained to hear more, but his father and the rider were walking away, out of range. His hand wrapped itself tightly around the small media player in his pocket. He didn't care about weapons, but he certainly didn't want to lose all of human technology. What were the elders planning?

He closed his eyes and pushed his anxiety away, returning to a calm state before he walked back to Mer with the salve and smoothed it into the small wound left by the splinter. He must not have been successful in keeping himself calm because Mer and the other dragons began to stir in their stalls with nervous energy.

He quickly finished his task, dropped the salve on the workbench, then bolted out of the stable, scrambled through the fence, and disappeared into the woods.

~~*

Avenall dashed down the trail to the clearing where Oriane made her home. When he got there, he saw her in the center of the glade. She sat slumped on the ground, her head held in her hands, her long black hair cascading over her face. When he drew nearer, he heard her sobs.

"Oriane? What's wrong?"

"It's my sisters. They're missing, and when I reached out to Euphemia today—the one the humans call Mona—she... she's been injured and is trapped in her nature form. I don't know if she can survive. She won't bleed from the wound as long she does not shift, and she'll be able to sustain herself that way for a while, but she will fade eventually if she can't transform to flesh. She will become a part of the forest as dryads do when they tire of their immortality. But Euphemia's human life has been so short. She wants to live."

"Do you know where she is? Can you send help?"

"No. I told you, Avie, my other sisters, none of them is connected to the earth. I can't feel any of them communicating. It's as if they no longer exist."

"Could it be that the elves have taken arms against the dryads, too? I was coming to ask you to send a message to the queen. I overheard my father say the dragons will be flying to war soon. The council plans on doing something to harm human technology. I don't know what it is, but Queen Lizbet needs to know the humans are to be attacked."

Oriane reined in her tears. "I can't get word to her without Euphemia. Can your human friend contact her?"

"I don't know. Humans have ways they can communicate quickly across distances, but she's a queen. Can someone unknown to her contact her if they desire? Surely she has guards?"

"But you must find a way to tell her how to find Euphemia! Soon it will be too late. I am selfish in this. I do not care about the elves going to war, I care only about my sweet sister. I will draw a map of the area where she is rooted. If they go to her with an experienced healer, her human body might be saved. My poor sister..."

Oriane tore a square of cloth from her gown and painstakingly sketched a map of a wooded area far across the sea with sap from a nearby tree while Avenall waited, thinking hard on the question of how he could contact a queen who was so far away. None of his ideas were very good. He was sure Danton would ask for something in return for the favor if he said he would be able to arrange it. Avenall had already given a dragon claw in exchange for his music and video machine. There were none left except the one he wore around his own neck on a chain, the symbol of the dragon tender. He could never part with that one. It had been Durian's before he left the compound. No, he could never part with Durian's gift, yet he had nothing left to trade. His other small possessions—a warrior's bow he would never use, an elaborately decorated sheath befitting the son of an elder, and other gifts he had been given before his magic made itself known—had already gone to Danton in trade. He hoped his friend would help from friendship alone this time.

Oriane finished her map, rolling it and tying it with a strip of twine. "You must get this to the queen, Avie. There is no one else. I'll run to the forest and join the trees, spending little time in this form. I hope they do not send a Magic Tracker for me, because I do not think I can run far enough to avoid one."

"Choose a part of the forest where dryads aren't know to dwell," Avenall replied, then grasped one of her hands with his. "Please hide yourself well. I would miss you so terribly if you were gone."

She smiled at this and leaned forward to kiss him on the cheek. "I will keep myself safe especially for you. You are good, Avie. I know you will not fail me."

She pulled her hand from his and ran gracefully into the heavy wood behind her. He watched until he could no longer glimpse her gown fluttering between the trees.

Avenall held aside the loose plank that allowed him to pass through the compound fence unnoticed. As he stuck his head through to survey the area before sneaking back in, his eyes were drawn to the opposite end of the compound. A large group was just entering the stone council house, and in the group, he saw a dryad being pushed toward the door, her feet bound with rope into a pair of thick leather boots. She would not be able to touch the earth.

Now he knew why Oriane could not contact her sisters. But what purpose could the elves have in capturing her? The dryads had never been enemies of the elves.

After the guards disappeared into the council house with the dryad, Avenall ran as swiftly as he could to the stable and climbed up into the small sleeping loft. He could hear the harsh breathing of the dragons below him, and he brushed against their minds quickly to assure himself that everything was well. Yes, all seemed well. Ashta, Fein, Gronda, Harul, and even Mer were settled in and content, no fears stalking their dreams. Good. It was good.

He dressed for bed and then tucked his sleeping fur around him for warmth, but he didn't find sleep. His thoughts returned to the map he'd placed in his pouch along with his media player and the other small treasures he had managed to keep secret. None of what he'd overheard that day or learned from Oriane made sense unless—was that the answer? The elves didn't want anyone to communicate with the queen. Whatever they were planning, they feared she could stop them.

After a while, Avenall gave up on sleep and exchanged his nightshirt for his day clothes. Making sure not to rouse the dragons by any sound, he snuck down the ladder from the loft and made his way from shadow to shadow toward the council house. He had to see for himself what they had done with the dryad, if he could.

Avenall had never tried to communicate mind to mind with another fae. It was forbidden on pain of death, and this ability that was whispered about among the farmers and herders was a myth. It had to be. And what dragon tender, a member of one of the lowest castes in society, would risk his life to find out if the myth was real? But there was no way for him to enter the council house except the front door. There were no windows into the cell where they must be holding her. It was his only choice even though it was a foolish and impossible one.

Avenall sank into the shadow against the rough stone of the council house wall. He placed his hands against it and tried to imagine the small room as it would look to a prisoner. His breathing grew shallow. He probed with his mind for the feel of thought mixed with magic and was rewarded by a small, bright spark on the other side of the wall.

It happened so easily. He closed his eyes, then looked out through the eyes of the other. She was in a small cage suspended from the ceiling of the cell. The floor of the cell, previously only dirt, had been lined from wall to wall with paving stone.

They meant to keep the dryad from the earth. At least they had not killed her.

And then he realized he had breached the mind of another fae. And still, he couldn't leave it without knowing. He sent a whisper.

"I am Avenall, Son of Shan. I am behind the wall at your back. You will not be able to see me, but I have come from Oriane. She has gone far into the forest, but she longs for word of her sisters."

He didn't know for a time if she'd heard him. The dragons responded only with emotion or movement. He didn't know what it would be like for a fae to respond to his whispers. He was nearly ready to leave as he chastised himself for believing ancient rumors when the softest of whispers sounded inside his head.

"A dragon tender? Then the myth is true. No wonder they keep you below them and tell you to stay in the stables. The elves must fear you terribly."

Avenall made no response. His brain worked to understand what she had just said. Could it be true? The elves feared the magic of the dragon tender?

"If you were sent by my sweet sister, then you are her Avie? She says you are quite beautiful for just a boy. I wish that I could see you. I am Placide."

He found himself blushing at her words. He was surprised by them, too. He hadn't known Oriane found him beautiful. Maybe she had noticed him in the way he wanted her to.

"She does call me Avie. I am him. Do you know why they've brought you here?"

"To keep us from communicating to the fae court and to the queen in her distant place. The elves want nothing of their actions here to reach her. A guard said the elves have all of my sisters captive in their dungeons in the high land. I am to be taken there on the new day, but I am glad that Oriane is not among them."

"But there are so many ways for the fae to communicate! They cannot stop them all."

"I don't know, Avie. Without Oriane and Euphemia, the queen will not have timely knowledge. I hope she is well guarded. I think the elves are not respecters of her position."

"It is as you say. The elves do not accept her." He thought for a moment. "I'm sorry I can't help you escape, but I've promised your sister I will tell all I know to the queen. Perhaps she will be able to retrieve you and your sisters from that place." He heard a scuffling around the corner of the building. "I have to go now. I will do what I can."

Avenall opened his eyes and moved quietly from the back of the council house to the building beyond it, traveling from shadow to shadow again until he reached the stable.

All was still. All was well. An elf might even imagine he is safe.

CHAPTER FOUR

A Change Is Gonna Come

RON ROSS SAT ACROSS the breakfast table from a silent daughter. Even when Tanji was the most upset with him, she usually forgave him quickly and began talking again before the end of the meal. This time, she kept her eyes on her food and responded to his questions with a "sure", a "whatever", or a shake of her head. It worried him.

Then, as she got up to clear the dishes and put them in the dishwasher, her voice sounded quietly from the kitchen, "Dad, would you be breaking up anyway if mom hadn't taken that job?"

He folded his paper, thinking carefully for a moment about his next words, "Yes. We've reached the end of our road. Obviously, I never wanted this to happen, but I'm glad it's finally out in the open. Pretending has been too hard for both of us. I knew she would eventually go when she accepted the initial contract out of state and wasn't home much." He took a long breath and let it out slowly before continuing. "Your mother has always been ambitious. She wasn't pleased when I decided to start a pest control company instead of continuing to look for something in business. She has higher aspirations than I do. I just like that I can now get home to dinner with you every night. Plus, I'm having the time of my life."

Tanji walked to where he sat and hugged him around the neck from behind. "I guess I knew something was wrong when Mom took the job out of state. Doesn't mean I can't hate it, though. Just don't gross me out by dating girls that aren't much older than me."

He smiled. "I think I can manage that."

Tanji sat down across from him, looking like she had something more to say, but she didn't start talking.

"Penny for your thoughts, sweetheart." *When in doubt, open with the cliché*, he thought.

"Dad, I...I think I made a mistake with Thomas. You were right about him being too old for me. Like, over a thousand years too old. I mean, he's interesting and smart and has a lot of talent with magic. Plus, he's hot looking. But he's such a party pooper. Sometimes it's like he was born without any fun in him at all."

"I'm sorry to hear it. You know I like Thomas. Given the difference in your ages, it was difficult for me to let you date him in the first place. But he always impressed me as a serious young man who wasn't out to make unreasonable demands on my baby girl."

"Sheesh, dad. Where's your head at? Thomas might as well still be a monk. He can't keep his mind off of magic long enough to try to compromise my situation. That's part of the problem."

"Good to know! Now I'm even more sorry to hear things aren't working out." He grinned at her, but she just narrowed her eyes in return.

"I haven't completely decided one way or the other. I still want to get him to talk about it, but he's so closed, you know? I never know what's going on inside his head."

"I can empathize. You know how your mother keeps things to herself until she explodes? But I don't think Thomas is the exploding type. He's locked down tight, as far as I can tell."

"Exactly. But I care about him, and somehow telling him that it's over seems like a really big deal, even though we haven't been together for that long. He takes it for granted we'll be together and acts like he doesn't have to work at it."

Ron listened as she expressed her frustrations. It took his mind off his own impending single-hood. When she'd talked it out, talking more to herself than to him, he asked, "You going to be okay at school today?"

"School? Yike! I'm never going to make it on time. Laters, pops." She grabbed her backpack and rushed for the door without another look.

It was nice to know that normal hadn't gone away completely.

Freoric leaned casually against a tree as the sun rose. The new light made the snow crystals on the forest floor twinkle like a field of frozen stars. It did not impress him. His eyes and ears were active, moving, ready for any threat. Not that there would be one here in this foreign patch of woods. Despite this, his training and sharp senses kept him ready for action even when there was no obvious cause: he heard the Abomination long before he arrived. Under the snow, the frozen leaves crunched as he walked, broadcasting his approach. He turned to watch Thomas moving toward him through the trees.

It was difficult not to show his disgust. He pretended pleasure as Thomas extended his hand for the handshake humans used in greeting, The custom began as the way a warrior showed he held no weapon against the other, although the humans had long ago forgotten this origin. What a stupid human custom. A warrior should never greet another unarmed.

He imagined his knife in his hand as he said, "It is good to see you, Thomas."

Thomas bowed his head and crossed his arms over his chest in the formal elven greeting. "It's good to see you, too, Freoric."

Freoric's expression remained impassive as he returned the greeting. "Have you news for me? The elders are eager for it."

"No, nothing really. According to James, the queen is still worried about the elves, but she hasn't done anything about it."

"Good. The half-dryad will no longer be passing information to her from the old world. This should stop the flow of rumors."

Thomas cocked his head and raised an eyebrow.

Freoric answered his unspoken question. "The dryad Euphemia has been silenced. It was necessary." If Freoric thought he'd pass the information on to other humans, he'd have ended him right then. But he wouldn't be so lucky today. Thomas showed no feeling.

"Walk with me now to keep us warm, Thomas. I have much to tell you."

Thomas fell in beside him as he turned, and they walked deeper into the woods, away from prying eyes.

CHAPTER FIVE
Angry Eyes

I N THE MORNING, AVENALL watched the rider move toward Harul with the bridle. He moved too quickly, startling the dragon, who jumped back despite Avenall's calming presence in her mind.

"Be careful, Evrard. Dragons are not horses. I may tend the dragons, but no one can command them. If you do not move slowly and allow the dragon to trust you, she will easily dispatch you before you've broken her to the saddle."

"Faugh. What do you know, dragon tender? Dragons exist to serve us. She'll bend to me no matter how I treat her." To make his point, he swung the bridle out, slapping the young dragon across her flanks. The leather made a popping sound as it made contact. Her scales would protect her from the sting of a leather strap, but Evrard was a warrior and had a warrior's strength. The bridle hit hard enough to cause pressure and make a loud smacking sound. She was young and easily frightened: Avenall barely prevented her from flaming. He did not know he had such strength in him.

He rounded on the dragon rider, stalking toward him threateningly and shouting, "Get out. Get out before I free their minds and let the dragons take you. These creatures are not your wife and children for you to beat. Leave before I let go and they do to you what is in their nature."

Evrard stood his ground defiantly, raising a hand to strike, but then dropped the bridle and backed away when a blast of smoke left Harul's snout. "Your father will hear of this insult, Avenall. Perhaps he will even allow me to wield the whip."

Avenall turned, dismissing him, as Evrard exited the training cage. He walked to Harul and stroked his hand gently along the side of her head where the red scales joined with the orange and yellow that covered the rest of her body. She was beautiful, like flame itself. He lay his head against her neck and sighed.

"Well, Harul, there will be no saddle for you today. But I think there might be one for me."

After shepherding Harul and the other dragons safely back to their stalls, Avenall climbed to the loft. He removed his leather jerkin and shirt, then slipped a black t-shirt with the human symbol "AC/DC" on the chest over his head. He put his shirt and leather jerkin back on over it and climbed out the back hatch of the loft. Within minutes, he was running through the forest in the direction of the village several miles away. If the council came for him, Oriane's message must already be on the way to the queen so that he was not prevented from delivering it.

Outside the town, he removed his shirt and jerkin again. He unbound his hair and left it loose on his shoulders in the human way which also hid his elven ears. He casually sauntered down the central street listening to his music. He hoped this would mark him as one of the humans who had adopted elements of elven dress rather than as an elf who risked imprisonment for adopting human ways.

Avenall walked the street, looking for the cafe where Danton said he worked. There, that was it. Avenall peered into the window of the brightly lit restaurant, scanning for his friend among the patrons. The crowd was small. Danton looked up just as Avenall located him. Danton's eyebrows lifted in surprise. Then he stowed the counter towel he held in his hand under the sink and walked to the door of the cafe.

"Mon ami, what are you doing here? Isn't it dangerous for you?"

"More dangerous than almost anything I have ever done," Avenall said, as he flashed back to Evrard backing out of the barn, anger and revenge in his eyes. "But I need your help. I have no one else to turn to."

Danton waved him inside. "Come, the break room." Avenall followed him into a small room with a tiny table and a few chairs crammed in with boxes of cups and lids behind it. Danton waved his hand at the chair on the left, "Go ahead, take a seat. I'm curious."

"I'm here to ask that you carry a message to the Queen of the Fae."

Danton laughed. "The Queen of the Fae, is it? You might as well ask me to carry a message to the Prime Minister of France. How would I accomplish that?"

"Humans have, what are they called? Phones?"

"Oiu, and if she's not listed, one of her friends might be. They aren't royalty. And there is always the mail or even email. So, perhaps it's possible to get a message to her." Danton looked cagily at Avenall. "You know nothing of the difficulties of these methods?"

"I do not. I could not use them. Will you help?"

Danton smiled, pleased he could turn the elf's lack of knowledge of modern communication into an opportunity once again. "I could do this for you, if it is important. But what will you give me in return?"

"I have nothing to give you except my thanks and friendship."

"Ah, that won't put money in the bank so that I can buy this place, will it? I don't plan on always doing the cleaning up. And the call will be expensive because it is such a long distance. That dragon claw you gave me sold well. Nearly four thousand euro. I could do it for another one of those, I think."

"I haven't got one."

"You have one around your neck."

"I can't give it up. Not for anything."

"Then I see you are on your own. We have nothing else to talk about." Danton stood and gestured toward the door of the small room, ushering Avenall out.

Avenall's heart was heavy as he walked through the town again, heading for the forest. The man he had thought was a friend had only been using him to collect elven keepsakes to sell. He had been no friend at all. Even worse, he still could not get a message to the queen. He would be nothing but a disappointment to Oriane. This hurt him even more now that he realized she and the dragons were the only friends he had left.

Maybe he should give up the dragon claw. It was, after all, just a dead piece of a dead dragon. Meaningless to anyone else. But Durian had given it to him, and Durian was the only elf who had treated him with kindness after the discovery that he would be a dragon tender. He would not betray the kindness and good memories of his true friend by selling the dragon claw for favors.

He wondered if all humans would treat him as Danton had done. If so, why should he even try to help their race? When he realized he was thinking like a good elven son to his father, it wasn't the cold day that made him shiver.

In the morning, Avenall was sure they would come for him, but no guards arrived with their swords drawn. No Elders came to the front of the stable to read charges.

He fed the dragons, cleaned their stalls, touched their minds, and found them contented and calm after yesterday's excitement. He rubbed each of them under their small, pointed ears, except for Fein, who disliked it and would pull away.

As the largest of the dragons, twice as large as a horse, Fein was the pride of the stable. He easily carried a rider for a day without rest, and he was the swiftest among them. Instead of rubbing Fein beneath the ears, he slipped him a special treat, a field mouse he had charmed into his hands especially for the dragon.

He couldn't bear it if the dragons were taken out among the humans as tools of death and objects of fear. In the wild, dragons kill for food or when they are frightened and need to protect themselves. Humans and fae are not their natural prey, but the elves press them into servitude as warriors. Avenall hated it, and he hated that it was his job to keep them calm while the warriors trained them to be tools for violence.

Evrard entered the stable, pulling Avenall abruptly from his thoughts.

"The elders have decided you are to be given another chance, but you will never dare to speak to me or any of your betters in the same way again, or I will lash you myself on the spot. Ready the dragons for training. The other riders will be arriving soon."

Avenall did as he was told that day. He had to focus on getting a message to the queen. He couldn't ruin that chance by losing his temper. He ignored the casual cruelty of the riders when the dragons did not do exactly as they demanded. He kept calming thoughts flowing through their minds whenever one of the herd spiked toward anxiety or fear. Despite this, it saddened him to watch Harul and Mer be put to bridle and saddle.

While he worked, his concern for both the dragons and his queen brought a plan to him that would allow him to fulfill his promise to Oriane.

Chapter Six
Turn Around, Look At Me

"Why all this interest in internal combustion and bombs all of a sudden? Wouldn't you rather be snuggled up with your girlfriend watching a romantic movie?" Tanji moved closer to him as she made her point, but Thomas continued to run a finger down the book that sat on the coffee table in front of him. His focus was intense. She wasn't even sure he'd heard her.

She got up and stamped off to the kitchen. "Nope. No. Let me just go ahead and answer that. You wouldn't rather be snuggled up with your girlfriend. Because you were a monk for all the right reasons."

Tanji took a tray of bottles and jars out of the cupboard and picked them up, read the labels, then set a few on the counter before she loaded the others back onto the tray and put it away. She took down the cobalt blue bowl she used as a mortar and blended the ingredients together carefully, measuring with a scale at times, pinching off a small amount at others.

When she was done, she walked to a spot about three feet behind the couch where Thomas sat. She took a handful of the mixture in the bowl and spread the powder through the air with a flowing gesture. Clouds formed at the ceiling and a small bolt of lightning, followed by an equally small clap of thunder, exploded in the corner of the room just before it started to rain heavily above Thomas's head. He slammed his book shut to try to keep it dry, but it was spattered with rain before he had it closed. He jumped up and turned to face Tanji, angry now.

"Why would you do that, you ignorant girl?" he shouted as fat raindrops continued to hit his face.

Tanji stayed calm despite her inner upset. "It was the only way I could think of to get your attention. But as it turns out, I don't want it. Get out, Thomas. It's done between us. Not that you'll notice." Thomas put his book down and moved to her, attempting an embrace as he apologized, but she pushed him away. "No. I'm sorry I pulled such a stupid trick, but it's not right between us anymore. I'll see you at work, and I'll see you as a friend, but I'm not your girlfriend any more, capisce?."

He nodded, gathered his books, and left. The storm Tanji had created followed him until it exhausted itself.

Tanji slumped down into the big, soft chair across from Lizbet's family room couch and threw her legs over one arm, flopping over to lounge across the other. She nodded her head at James when he looked up from keeping his eye on Bobby's moves in the video game.

James gave an acknowledging nod in return and turned his attention back to the game. Lizbet sat across from her, cheering her brother on.

"Your former roomie is a freak, you know?" Tanji lobbed at James. "He'd rather study than spend time with a beautiful woman."

James gave a half-smile without removing his attention from the TV screen. "Well sure, who wouldn't?"

"Really, he's made me nuts for the last time. I ended it." She turned to Lizbet then, not really meaning to include James in the first place, but it felt good to send some of her anger in a male direction. "I just hope it isn't uncomfortable at work. Not like he'll notice me any more than he ever did. Yeah...not going to be uncomfortable at all, really."

"Did you for sure break up?" Lizbet asked. "You're not just saying you're going to do it and then decide he's all cute and smart and not annoying at all? And I'll be in trouble for dissin' on your boyfriend if I say you can do better?"

"Yeah, yeah...I really did it. And I mean it. I just hope my dad doesn't pop a blood vessel when he sees the storm damage in the living room."

"Huh? Storm damage?"

"I can get creative. Just a little thunder and lightning..."

Lizbet laughed. "You did a rainmaking spell *inside* your house? Really?"

Tanji tried not to grin, but she couldn't help herself. "I know, right? It was uber-cool, girl. You should have seen it. And, you know, super-metaphorical. I'm going to carry a storm around with me in a pouch from now on."

"Thanks for the warning. I'll start carrying an umbrella. But I can't say it bothers me you dumped him. I don't care what James says, and I don't care about all that time you've spent trying to convince me that Thomas is okay, I still don't trust him. And I'm never going to like him. Makes my day that you're not going to insist on dragging him out with us on double-dates anymore."

"Yeah, well, that was the daddio's rule, not mine. He was convinced we needed a chaperone. Difference in ages and all that. He has big trust for James narcing if Thomas acted like a bad boy. Like he would, right?"

As Tanji spoke, Sheila Moore walked into the family room from the garage. "Oh, a houseful, I see."

"Hey Mom. How was dinner with Mona?" Lizbet called from the sofa. Bobby just nodded quickly then returned his attention to James's navigation through the battlefield.

"She didn't turn up. It's so unlike her. I called her, but she didn't answer. I had dinner anyway since the restaurant was booked, and I kept hoping she'd get there, but I can't think what's happened. I'm sure it's nothing."

"Yeah, right, Mom. 'Cause everything around here turns out to be nothing. Plus, she was supposed to give me a call just to help me keep up with what's going on in Europe until my weekend visit to court, but she didn't. And that is also really not like her. Bobby, hey, would you like me to..."

Bobby didn't even turn away from his game to say, "Make me a bowl of ice cream, right? Because every time you start talking all fairy-secrets, I get a bowl of ice cream and have to eat it somewhere else. Like I don't know."

"Well, yeah. So, I guess you're not interested in ice cream?"

"I didn't say that! I just said I know what you're doing. I'm not dumb."

He followed her into the kitchen, and she dropped a

couple of sisterly noogies on his head before she handed him his treat.

James held his hand out in front of him, following the glowing dot as it traversed a map across his palm which wrote and revised itself in brilliant color as they traveled. They'd walked about half a mile from their starting point near Mona's apartment when the orb stopped moving and changed from blue to gray, then disappeared. The woods were suddenly much darker than they'd been before.

James looked around, and said, "So, we're in the middle of the woods and the spell says she's here, but I don't see her. Maybe this spell doesn't always work the way I thought it would."

Tanji and Lizbet scattered in opposite directions, ranging away from where James stood, to see if Mona was anywhere near, but they found nothing. There was still an inch or two of snow on the ground from the day before, but there were no footprints in it to show Mona had come this way. But it was dark, and the starweed Tanji used to light the area didn't bring the light up that much.

When the girls returned, James rubbed his palms together and ended the spell. He took mittens out of his coat pocket and shoved his hands in quickly against the cold. "I don't get it. The spell works for me whenever I want to find something I've lost. It always gets me within at least ten feet. It should have worked to find Mona, too, if she's in range. If she's not, it shouldn't light up at all."

"Maybe she's shielding herself magically?" said Tanji.

Lizbet shook her head. "I can't think of a single reason she'd do something like that. I mean, she and my mom are close. Like grownup besties close. If she needed to hide for some reason, my mom would know. Man, I hate this. Nothing about it feels right."

Tanji said, "I'm there with you—my spidey-sense is way tingly right now. Having one of super-wizard Myrddin's spells lead us nowhere is a bad sign."

James shrugged. "I don't always get it right." He started to walk toward Lizbet, reaching out his hand to take hold of hers in preparation for the walk back, but he stumbled, tripping on something under the snow. He bent over and brushed it clear. "Guys, what kind of shoes does Mona wear?" He stood and handed the snowy shoes to Lizbet so she could take a closer look.

"Yep, I think these are hers. She likes slip-ons, even in the winter, so she can get them off fast and connect to the earth. I guess your spell didn't go completely wrong after all. But, so...where's Mona?"

She swept her eyes around again, but all she could see was tree after tree.

～～*

Sheila clicked the off button on the remote when she heard the front door open. "Did you find her?"

Lizbet walked into the family room, shaking her head. "No. Just these." She held up the shoes.

"Those are hers. She wears them with that long green skirt all the time."

"Yeah, that's what I thought. We found them in the woods. But that's all. I'm trying not to get crazy about it, but I need to go to Scotland to find out if the dryads at the court have heard from her. I wish a few more of the fae would get with it like Eamon and start a cell phone family plan. I'll go tomorrow after school."

"No, not tomorrow. As much as I'm concerned about Mona, I don't want you to get stuck there and miss dinner. Your father is joining us, and I want the two of you to make nice to each other. I've had enough of this cold front between you. It's time to get it straightened out, and since he's agreed to come by, you're going to be here."

Lizbet started to protest, but her mother stopped her. "No arguments. I divorced the man, but we manage to speak to each other civilly. Plus, while I'm at it, I don't want you going alone to Scotland, either. You need to take James or Eamon with you."

"Fine. I'll ask James. Is Saturday morning okay?"

"Sure. I'm as anxious for news of Mona as you are, I'm just not sure you're going to find it in Scotland. I'm pretty sure if you thought so, you'd be there right now."

"Well, it is the middle of the night over there."

"Because that would stop you? I know you better than that."

Lizbet knew she was right. "No. Being queen has its perks. It's not like anyone would complain if I woke them up. You're sure she didn't say anything to you that might help us figure this out?"

"I've been over everything she's said to me in the past month, sweetie. Things were just normal—as normal as things can be for a half-dryad, I guess. She loves working for Ron. She's enjoying getting to know the other dryads in Europe, and she gets so excited when she talks about how they communicate through the earth. I mean, there was nothing going on with her that seemed out of place."

When she got out her homework to study before bedtime, Lizbet had a hard time staying focused on verb tenses.

If there was nothing about Mona's life that would have caused her to disappear, then either something completely random had happened, or something *fae* had happened. She was hoping for "oops, I forgot to tell you all I'd be visiting my mom" or something equally harmless. And then they'd all have a laugh for having gotten themselves bent out of shape about it, and that would be lots better than the alternative. Because anything fae always turned out to be trickier than it appeared on the surface.

CHAPTER SEVEN
No Place Like Home

ELDER SHAN SCOWLED IN distaste as he scanned the scene in front of him. "These humans, they hover around us like flies to carrion. I am tired of seeing them outside the gate. Scatter them and make sure they do not return. I see no reason to be delicate."

The archer at his side behind the parapet nodded and nocked an arrow. He sighted for a long time, choosing his target with care. When he loosed the arrow, it flew true to pierce the meaty part of a man's upper leg where he stood at the front of the small crowd of people. He crumpled, screaming.

Another human male, who wore an imitation of elven attire, moved closer to the gate, shouting, "What's wrong with you? Why would you do something like that?"

The response was an arrow to the chest.

People scrambled down the path, frantic, some stepping

over others, some stopping to help the fallen. Shan smiled to himself as the man who had challenged the elves slowly bled to death outside the compound.

~~*

An ambulance arrived and drove directly to the injured man, opening the back door away from the direction of the fortress. It also picked up the one with the arrow through his chest, but he was cold now, beyond help.

After the ambulance sped away, a white van with a satellite transmitter on top drove cautiously up the road. It stopped just outside arrow range. Once it was parked, the TV crew disembarked. The cameraman pointed his camera toward the fortress gate while the sound technician pointed a long-range mic in the same direction. The reporter straightened his tie and lifted a megaphone.

"We want to talk to you. You fired on your fans today."

There was no response from the fortress. Nothing stirred.

"Please, we only want to talk. Tell us why you attacked. We want to understand."

The Elder appeared on the catwalk above the gate, hold-ing onto his staff, his appearance composed and majestic, his long brown hair bound tightly with a leather cord in a elven braid that he had pulled over his left shoulder. He held the elder's staff in his other hand. It ended at his eye level in a carved insignia of his office. He was impressive in any culture.

"The elves have grown tired of human interference. We've asked you to leave us alone in the past, and yet you cannot even keep your people from making camp outside our gates. Now, perhaps, you will."

The live feed went out to Paris and was translated and rebroadcast to the world within minutes.

When she got home from school, a young queen's heart raced wildly as she watched the news report.

After listening to his father's speech from behind the crowd of riders and warriors gathered at the gate, Avenall hurried back to the stable.

He used all of his power to remain in each of the dragon's minds at the same time. He imagined for them a long flight over the forest, then over the seas, then landing in a new world where there would be no elves and no dragon riders. He withdrew at last, after each of the dragons had agreed to take the journey. Although they could not communicate with language, they understood his emotion and the pictures he made for them.

Avenall climbed to the loft and collapsed onto the bed of straw that served as his mattress. It had tired him to be with all the dragons at once. He wanted to take them away now, but it would be safer to leave at night, and he would be better prepared if he was able to get a little sleep. He hoped the TV crew outside the gates had been wise enough to go away after his father's pronouncement.

He now believed that the elves would soon be going to war, but it would be a foolish war they could not win. What spirit of self-destruction possessed them? Did they wish to be destroyed? No war was a good war, but this one *must* be prevented.

Avenall woke refreshed at dusk. He fed the dragons and then urged them to eat more when they'd finished. They would need to store as much energy for the flight as they could. It would be many days before they arrived in the queen's land. He still was not sure how they would rest or feed on the journey. If they could not easily gain their sustenance from the sea and rest without the availability of land, they'd have to turn back. And then where would he go? He would no longer have a home, only the promise of death in any elven compound he arrived at. And where could he hide the dragons in his own land that the elves could not recapture them?

He prepared one saddle for his personal use and set it down near Fein's stall. He placed saddles near the smaller dragons as well, but these he loaded with packs containing food, furs, and his meager possessions. He slipped out of the stable and into the armory, where he took as many waterskins as he could carry. It would not be enough water for the dragons, but they could drink the brine of the oceans for their needs. Their stomachs would not reject it like his would.

All of the dragons but Mer accepted their burden without complaint. In Mer, he sensed discomfort with the new sensation of weight on his back and also a fear of the vast expanse of ocean he had seen when Avenall shared his mind. Avenall knew it would tax him, but he quickly shared with Mer the vision in Fein's memories of the ocean where the other dragons had flown when the fae were freed. Mer calmed with Fein's memories of the freedom he experienced so far away from stables and cages.

"What are you doing, boy?" someone said behind him. He turned, and Evrard stood there, glaring at the saddled dragons, hand on the hilt of his sword, ready to act.

Inside, Avenall tensed with fear. On the outside, he stood tall with bravado. "Nothing that concerns you, dragon rider." The dragons, still tenuously connected to his thoughts, shifted restlessly in their stalls.

He was upset to see Evrard there, just when he thought they would escape without challenge. He felt Fein prepare for conflict. He was having trouble maintaining the ease he needed to keep his charges calm.

He might as well take a chance. He'd already prepared to leave everything he'd ever known behind. This treason alone would earn him a sentence of death. He had nothing else to lose.

He lowered his head, took a deep breath, blew it out quickly, then looked directly into the dragon rider's eyes. As he did, he aggressively pushed a suggestion in a way he would never do with dragons.

Evrard's expression went blank, then he turned and walked out of the stable toward the armory, where he disappeared inside. Avenall watched him until he was gone. He hoped the rider was now lying on the weapon-building table fast asleep. It would allow them more time to get away before the alarm was raised.

He led the dragons out of the stable, then asked Fein to bend down so that he could mount. He'd never mounted a dragon before. A dragon tender's place is on the ground. He gasped as the dragons took the sky and the compound where he'd lived all his life fell away from him forever.

Avenall looked out to the horizon and saw only darkness ahead beneath the stars, the sky meeting the water in a dark blur far in the distance. He borrowed Fein's superior sight to guide them toward a stony beach on a small island. He didn't know if they would see land again soon. When he was honest with himself, he didn't know if they would ever see land again.

They'd been flying for many hours, and he was glad that the dragons still weren't showing signs of tiring. He hoped they'd landed unnoticed so they could remain here for the night and continue on in the morning. It would take nearly a full span of days to reach the American queen after they set off across the sea.

Although he knew the world was wider than the small forest in which he had spent his entire life, he still could not comprehend the vastness of it; the water went on forever as he looked out away from the land.

Mer bumped his head against Avenall's back. The tap was not meant to cause harm, but it was strong enough that it nearly sent him sprawling. He peered into the young dragon's mind and immediately understood that he wanted his saddle removed. Avenall undid the cinch and lifted the saddle off. Mer quickly sprawled over onto his side to scratch his back against the stony ground.

Avenall busied himself removing all of the saddles and looked to the dragons, sending an image of Fein pulling fish from the sea with his massive jaws. As he pictured it, the dragons took flight as one, each of them skimming out over the seas and then diving like ducks to come up again with a wriggling fish clenched between their teeth. They returned to the rock and dropped their dinners, going back for more until there was a moving silver mass near where each of them landed.

Avenall looked longingly at the fish as the dragons filled their bellies, wishing he had a fire and a fishing line for himself. It did not occur to him to take what was not his from the dragons. He hadn't meant to share this thoughts, but Fein turned toward a rocky cleft where a cache of vegetation had caught and dried. The dragon breathed a burst of fire and the dried vegetation began to burn. Avenall quickly moved to fan it to greater flame. Fein tossed a fish from his pile toward him. Avenall wondered whose mind was in whose as he gathered strands of damp seaweed to wrap his fish so that it didn't blacken in the coals.

He slept well that night with a full stomach.

CHAPTER EIGHT

Sea Cruise

THEY STOPPED TO FEED the next day after long hours of flight. The younger dragons brought fish they tossed to Fein as he circled their hunting ground, unable to join them because he carried Avenall. Avenall felt bad about that, but it is a rare elf who learns to swim. If he ever got the chance, he would gladly take it up: he'd followed the dragons' minds into the sea as they streaked through the water, and there was a clear sense of joy as they swam. He silently apologized to Fein for preventing him from joining the others in their pleasure.

Avenall shivered and wrapped himself tighter into the furs he wore for warmth. The cold crept into his bones. The inner fire of the dragons warmed them, but he was not built for long exposure to this weather. As he shivered, he felt a spike of emotion from the dragon beneath him.

Avenall had thought he understood the vastness of the

ocean before they set off from the island that morning, but now, twelve hours into their flight, he felt the tired ache in the dragons' wings. He shared their urge to sleep and rest from the long voyage. But there was nowhere to rest. No land, no drift, nothing solid where they could sleep before continuing.

When the dragons finished feeding, Fein led them again through the sky, but in a different direction than before. Confused, Avenall reached for the dragon's mind and was surprised to see an image of himself there, huddled beneath his furs, face pale and pinched with the cold. Fein sent him a thought of warmth as he bore left, away from their original path, just as the sun began to set. A few hours later, the cold was less severe and he was able to find a little sleep sprawled forward onto the dragon's wide neck.

Night had given way to dawn when he sensed a change in the unending blue in Fein's mind. The dragon had spotted something on the horizon, something that was not the sea. It was small, but it was getting bigger. Avenall was soon able to see the speck on the horizon with his own eyes. Fein turned toward the object, and Avenall relinquished his suggestion to hold back, letting the dragon take the lead. He knew they all needed a place to rest.

The speck on the horizon grew closer swiftly. Soon, Avenall could make out the shape of a boat. One much larger than any his people had described in their stories. It was a floating castle with hundreds of people on the roof. As Avenall watched, some of them spotted the dragons and rushed to the side of the ship where the dragons approached.

Avenall was only a little concerned for the safety of these people. As long as they did not attack or threaten the dragons, there was little danger. But he was not sure that landing on such a vessel was a good idea. Was it a ship of war? He had no way of knowing.

He sent a suggestion to Fein to fly in circles around the ship while he looked for the best place to land. At the highest level, there was a pool of water next to a large round chimney from which waves of heat disturbed the air. In rows around the pool, humans reclined, some holding books. Others appearing to be sleeping. It was the least populated area, and the easiest one on which to land. He directed the younger dragons to make another circuit around the ship while he guided Fein to land atop the chimney.

As Fein headed for the suggested perch, one of the reclining men below spotted him, and started calling out to the people around him, "hey, dragons...there's dragons!"

The others looked where he pointed, gathered up their possessions hurriedly, and ran as a group down the stairs leading away from the upper deck of the boat. Some looked back over their shoulders in fear. Avenall would have tried to assure them that dragons are not aggressive by nature, but in this case, he was glad they ran away. His dragons were, although he did not like to think of them as such, battle-trained. They were also tired and moody after their long flight. Avenall didn't need anyone frightening them into defensive behavior.

Fein perched on the chimney until the last of the humans had gone. Then he glided smoothly from his perch to the deck, where Avenall dismounted. Fein moved then to the pool and dipped his snout to take a drink. He drew it back quickly, letting the water he'd sucked up dribble out between his teeth. He snorted, and a whiff of smoke curled out, but he kept his flame under control.

Avenall bent to the pool and cupped his hands to bring some of the water to his lips. He dipped his tongue into it and immediately uncupped his hands in disgust. There was something wrong with this water. He removed a waterskin from Fein's saddle and took a long drink to rid himself of the awful taste. He patted the dragon's neck and spoke soothingly. "This water is spoiled, my friend. You will need to continue drinking from the sea."

Avenall looked to the sky and directed his thoughts toward the rest of the dragons, who were still making a tight circle high above his head. They slowly circled down to claim their places on the boat. Mer perched on the chimney to watch the people on the lower deck. Asta, Gronda, and Harul took roosts on the railing, looking toward the water, their sharp eyes darting here and there, and their minds full of thoughts of a fish dinner. He gave them leave to begin fishing, and they soared out over the sea immediately. Fein remained with Avenall.

A man dressed all in white walked up the stairs to the level where Avenall stood. He paused at the top of the stairs, hesitating as his eyes moved from Avenall to Fein. Then he walked forward again, hand extended. Avenall blinked and sent a request to Fein, who turned and walked to the end of the boat, then hunkered down while keeping a watchful eye on them.

Avenall extended his hand to clasp the one that was offered to him. He waited for the man to speak and hoped he knew his language.

"I'm Captain Collins. This is my ship," the man said slowly.

Avenall understood. He hoped his English would serve him. He had only ever been able to practice it with Oriane. "I am called Avenall. These are my dragons," he said with a slight gesture of his hand toward the herd.

The Captain smiled a broad smile, friendly.
Avenall smiled back. It was a good start.

CHAPTER NINE

Daddy's Home

S HAN DISPLAYED NO EMOTION as the master of the dragon riders informed him of Avenall's theft. It was too late now to do anything to prevent the boy's treason. He'd been gone when the dragon riders arrived for morning training. The loft had been searched, and the boy had taken all of his possessions with him.

Shan moved to dismiss the other man with a gesture, but the master of the dragon riders said, "I have one more urgent subject to speak to you about. But it must be in absolute secrecy. It is a matter for the council, not for the people."

Shan nodded his head at each of his assistants, indicating they should leave the room. "Speak, then. As if you could bring me any worse news than what you have already relayed."

"One of the riders, Evrard, went to the stable last night

to confront Avenall after his defiant behavior. He remembers nothing after that confrontation until he woke up on the weapons-building table in the armory when I entered to see if anything had been taken."

Shan didn't speak. If he had tried, his rage would have choked him. It had been over a thousand years since a dragon tender had been born with the ability to enter higher minds. No one must know that it had happened again.

He composed himself. "Master Rider, who other than you and Evrard know of this?"

"Only the two of us, Elder."

"Good. You will keep this secret."

When his inferior had been gone for a safe period of time, Shan began to fume, overturning furniture and bringing the decorative weapons crashing down from their shelf. He should have drowned the boy when he was a elfling. He should have had him beaten for his disrespect to Evrard, but the council had stayed his hand. He'd agreed not out of affection but because the compound had no other dragon tender. No one could fill his role if he'd died or needed time to recover from his injuries.

Shan stormed out of his study and barked at a waiting servant to clean up the mess he left behind. He went to gather the members of the council and inform them of the folly they had wrought.

He would take joy in swinging the sword at the boy's beheading.

~~*

Oriane stumbled in the too-large, heavy leather boots the elves had bound to her feet and fell roughly to the ground.

"Get her up. Don't let her catch onto the ground, we'll have to chop her down to get her into the cell!"

Rough hands grabbed her on each side and forced her to stand. The chains that hung from her wrists caught under her knees for a long moment, scraping painfully against her slender wrists.

From the excited voices around her, she understood she was a prize for them. She had been a known friend of the dragon tender. She might even have helped him in his treason. She might even know where he'd taken the dragons.

It didn't matter to her how much she hurt or how much she was humiliated by their treatment of her: she'd learned from her captors something that made her heart sing. Avie had escaped and was on his way to find the queen. She bore their rough handling with a smile. Her sister, Euphemia, might still be saved.

The guards dragged her along through the gates of the compound, and the elves who gathered along their route spit on her and jeered. However, one or two of them, those from the lower castes, looked ashamed and sorry for it even as they humiliated her.

Soon, it ended. The guards placed her in an iron cage that hung suspended from the ceiling of a cell in a back room of the council house.

Oriane kept her secret, although she lost her smile when Shan began to tear the living, feeling branches from her scalp one by one by one.

Her screams gave nothing away.

~~*

At the dinner table, Lizbet filled her mother in on the search for Mona. "So, we've been looking for two days, but we're not finding. I mean, James used a locator spell the first day, and we found her shoes, but that's it. So she either disappeared into thin air or she's hiding from us. If she's in her nature form, we'd never recognize her. A tree's a tree, right?"

Lizbet's father stopped eating and said, "What do you mean a tree's a tree? I thought you were looking for a person? Is this some fae nonsense again?"

Lizbet had almost forgotten her father was there. She'd been ignoring him so well since the start of the meal. She still wasn't sure she was ready to patch things up. He'd made it pretty clear what he thought of the fae and magic. She wasn't going to go around apologizing for who she was so her father would accept her. "Mona is a dryad, dad...well, a half-dryad. She can transform from person-shaped to tree-shaped. She came here from Texas looking for me after Fae Day and decided to stay. She works for Mr. Ross now, and she's good friends with mom. So, if you say something mean about her being able to turn into a tree, you'll just make both of us mad."

For a moment, his eyesbrows pulling down a fraction, his mouth beginning to clench, vur then it relaxed. "I deserved that, I guess. And I think I know who you're talking about now. Is she the Asian woman who wears the twigs and leaves in her hair?"

"Yep, except the twigs and leaves are *part* of her hair, so no choice on wearing them. It's not just a fashion statment." Lizbet took a deep breath, shrugged a small shrug, and continued, "Look, sorry I was all judgy and went off on you. I know you're trying."

Her father grinned. "Maybe you actually did inherit a little something from me."

Bobby chimed in, "Oh she did, Dad. She really did."

Bobby didn't understand why his serious statement was

funny, but when everyone else started laughing, he laughed along with them.

Still laughing, Lizbet shook her fork at him and said, "I'm so going to get you back for that one!"

She suddenly realized she loved having all of her family around again. She'd spent a lot of time being upset at her father for not being perfect, but she'd missed this.

CHAPTER TEN

Where Have You Gone

O N SATURDAY MORNING, LIZBET materialized with James in tow just in front of the small, stone throne in the main room of the fae's Scottish castle. It was completely silent. She let go of James's hand and walked to a side room, hoping to find someone—one of the dryads or the naiads or even a centaur or one of the elves. But there was no one there.

Her past lives flashed memories of ancient enemies and furious battles in her head. *Knock it off. I don't have time or energy for all your predictions of doom.* The flashes of memory stopped. She took a deep breath and looked over to James. "So, does Myrddin have any suggestions, or is he as much of a doom and gloom guy as Morgan and her buddies?"

"He hasn't got any more of a clue than I have. I say we look around outside."

They exited the keep to the gardens, and it was clear

that something had happened there. Lizbet looked out over what was once a well-maintained formal landscape. Now, plants were crushed or torn up. But other than that, nothing. It was a peaceful scene. It made no sense that there was no one there.

A slight sound behind her made her turn. James must have heard it, too, because he turned with her. A small figure darted from behind a hedge and took off running toward the forest. James held up his hand and beckoned toward the being who, despite still running furiously in the other direction, began to move slowly toward him.

Eventually, the being realized he'd been caught and looked back toward his captor, fright showing in his large, wide eyes. Then he relaxed, turned, and allowed himself to be drawn along. "Och, I didn't recognize ye, my queen. And Myrddin, too. Have you brought Eamon with ye? He'd be a sight for sore eyes about now."

Lizbet recognized Eamon's brother gruagach. "It's Hamish, isn't it? You're Eamon's friend."

James released his magical hold and the gruagach made a low bow.

"I am that, my queen. Can you take me to him? Because I dinnae want to stay here any longer than I have to. I was only hidin' until I was sure the elves were gone."

"Elves did this?"

"Aye, and a fine clean up job they did after. There should have been some blood about. The Centaurs took heavy casualties, but do you see their bodies? No. The elves took them and scattered a bit of magic about to hide what happened. The dryads they took away in chains. Most of the rest of the fae folk escaped when one of your sister auraes had them form a chain and blew a great load of pixie dust around the room. I declined to join them and took my place with the centaurs to help hold your castle. I'm afraid I dinnae do a very good job of it." Hamish hung his head, suddenly overcome.

Lizbet squatted down to be level with the gruagach and gently reached out to lift his head and look into eyes that were beginning to tear up in the corners. "Hamish, there's no doubt in my mind that you were very, very brave. Of course we'll take you with us."

The gruagach cheered at this. "Thank you. I couldnae bear to be alone here in this field of tragedy much longer."

* ～ * ～ *

Hamish sat center stage in the Moore's living room. He munched contentedly on liberally buttered popcorn and handfuls of cheese puffs as he began the tale of what he now referred to as the "Battle for the Highlands Court".

"We didn't expect a thing, ye ken? None of the court elves had been actin' strange until suddenly they're popping out from all corners, pulling everyone together with a caging spell. It was a powerful one, too, well beyond the power of any elven wizard I've ever known..." he nodded at James, "...present company excluded, of course."

James nodded his head minutely to indicate acknowledgement. Hamish bolted down another handful of cheese puffs, then continued.

"Well, that's when you would have thought the gates to the other world were opening! Outside, you could hear the elven horns and the centaurs shouting to each other to arm as quickly as they could. The nymph Aisha, she beckoned everyone close who was trapped in the caging circle and had them hold hands. I'd just come in from the stables so I was outside the circle. Someone reached a hand to me through the cage, but I didn't take it. I knew I had to stay and defend us. Then Aisha threw great handfuls of pixie dust into the air, and suddenly they were gone. I don't know where she took 'em."

"I ran outside, and the elves had already captured the dryads who'd made for the woods. They wrapped their legs in boots and chains and then they took them away. Montan—you know him, Eamon, a good fae—he'd never give a kickin' to anyone who dinnae well and truly deserve it. He lifted me onto his back, handed me a mace, and to battle we went. We got some licks in with those elves, but just as quickly as we took one down, a blast of magic would come from the side, and he'd be healed and back up again. I can't explain it. I've never seen nothin' like it. There must have been a powerful wizard on the side of the elves, although I never saw one—only those magical blasts come from nowhere. And the stench! It was near as powerful as the magic. The only time I've ever noticed such a strong, musky smell was when I came upon a group of fauns in the deep wood. Do ye ken? The sons of Bacchus may be with the elves."

Lizbet patted James's shoulder to get his attention and gave him a questioning look. He mouthed the word "later" in return. She turned her attention back to Hamish's story.

"Montan went down..." Hamish dropped his head, took a few deep breaths, and then raised it again, "...but I was able to jump clear, and I'm ashamed to say I ran back to the garden and hid myself down a gnome hole. We'd lost anyway. The centaurs were all of them captured or killed. And someone had to be left to tell the tale." Hamish stopped then and swept a dirty cuff across the corner of one eye, where a tear had started to form. "He was a good fae, that Montan, a good fae."

Sheila, who'd been listening with tears in her own eyes, impulsively rose and went toward the gruagach to comfort him with a hug. He lifted his small hands to stop her and said, "No need for emotional stuff, no, no...but maybe just a bit of what the lad's havin'?"

Sheila said, "Of course," and hustled into the kitchen to get another bowl of ice cream, followed by both the gruagach and her son, who didn't want to be left out if more ice cream was being offered.

CHAPTER ELEVEN
I've Got My Eyes On You

AFTER THE OTHERS LEFT for the kitchen, James wrapped his arm around Lizbet. She snuggled into his side and said, "The thing is...Mona's half dryad, and based on what Hamish saw, it seems like the elves are going after the dryads. Now that I know that, her disappearing is just getting more and more scary. And, despite how much he sucks up to me, Freoric is the only elf in this country that we know about, so that puts him right there as the top suspect, don't you guys think?"

Eamon paced back and forth with his hands folded behind his back. A serious expression darkened his already unattractive face, "Aye, I agree it would have to be Freoric, but we've found nothing to prove the dryad's come to harm. We can't go accusin' him. We've got to have something solid."

"Any ideas how to get that?" asked James.

"We need one of those spy networks your human governments are so fond of."

Lizbet rolled her eyes, "No problem, I've got one in my backpack. Really."

"I was thinking backyard, more likely," Eamon said without a hint of humor.

Lizbet looked puzzled for a moment, then her eyes lit up, and she grinned. "The gnomes. Who would suspect them of having anything to do with intelligence?" she asked, as she raised her hands and put air quotes around the word intelligence. "That's actually kind of brilliant."

Eamon stood taller at that. "Aye, you know I don't like to blow my own horn, but I'll not disagree."

James shifted to lean in closer to Eamon and took his arm from around Lizbet. She sat up straighter, more alert now that a plan was developing. Lizbet enjoyed listening to her boyfriend and her lives-long friend plotting and planning. Their last plan had been both creative and effective. The fact that she was back in control of her own body instead of still under the control of her fae half was proof of that.

"How're you going to keep the gnomes focused long enough to get any information gathering out of them?"

"That's where the sorcery comes in, is it not? Surely Myrddin or Morgan can come up with a way to supercharge a group of gnomes long enough to get decent spy work out of them."

James rubbed his chin. "It could work. Might need Tanji for this, though. That book of hers is awfully useful. And Thomas..."

Lizbet interrupted him. "Not Thomas. Not this time. Not when it has to do with Freoric or the elves. You know how he feels about them."

"Okay, but I just thought by pooling minds and talents..." He stopped when he noted Lizbet's warning look. "...but, yeah, okay, I'm not going to argue on that one. So, we have to think of something that won't harm them in any way but makes them act a little less gnome-like for a while. Plus," James said, turning back to Eamon, "and this is a big point for me—they need to agree to it. I'm not dosing them up without them knowing about it. This isn't like when they tried to make Bobby their king or god or whatever they thought he was. They've behaved since then, and they were a big help with the fae Morgan, so we owe them some respect. This is a whole different situation."

"Right. The day you find me respectin' a gnome..."

Lizbet stopped him. "James is right, Eamon."

Eamon replied, "As you say, mistress," but his eyes continued to disagree.

Thomas placed the large glass globe on top of the metal stand. He'd shaped it with magic and scrap metal he'd nicked from an abandoned building. The large globe came from a local glassblower. It had to be magic-free so that it didn't absorb any of the magical essence it would soon contain. It had cost most of a month's salary but had just the right symmetry to collect and concentrate the wisps. It would also be nicely concealed in the woods by the old cement silo near the abandoned railroad tracks.

He was pretty sure a group of dusters used the silo as a meeting spot. That would have to stop: the repelling spell he'd devised should give anyone coming too close a deep sense of unease and prevent them from entering. If someone did fight the fear and get too close for his comfort, they'd regret it when they found it harder and harder to breathe. By the time anyone was near enough to the silo to potentially cause trouble, their heart would be racing with anxiety and they'd soon pass out from lack of oxygen. Thomas wasn't leaving this one to chance.

He completed the protection spell, then began the larger ritual. James called his talent for combining two or more spells "magical macgyers". He wasn't sure what that meant, but he felt certain James approved of his talent. Too bad he couldn't tell him about this one.

He interweaved the various threads of magic, focusing intently and visualizing each of the spells as a strand of blue power, tweaking this one here, that one there, and then weaving them into a coherent whole. He couldn't suppress a satisfied if somewhat smug smile. He congratulated himself on the thorough job he'd done planning and the ease with which he'd worked the complex magic.

Around the world, the wisps felt a tug at their magical core, an irresistible attraction to a single point on the map. Wherever they were, they turned and made a beeline for Ohio.

CHAPTER TWELVE
Today We Heard The News

"RIGHT, SO HERE'S THE plan," Eamon said to the four gnomes lined up in front of him in Lizbet's back yard. "You'll follow that elf, Freoric. The assassin, right?" He paced and glared as he spoke. "If you keep your mind on the job and bring us back good information, there's a reward. An entire bag of sugar—not one shared by the huddle—a full bag for each of you."

Behind Eamon, James held up a bag of sugar for the gnomes to see. He had to put it down again when the gnomes got distracted, leaning slightly toward the treasure with glazed expressions on their faces, forcing Eamon to turn around and scold, "Och, like that's helping. What can you be thinkin'?"

When Eamon turned around again and slapped his walking stick against the ground to regain the gnomes' attention, James smirked. Something about hanging out with the gnomes made him feel like he was Bobby's age and his only job was to have fun. Sometimes, he even indulged himself in a gnome game or two when no one was looking, pretending he joined in for Bobby's sake, but really, who doesn't want to play King of the Hill with a bunch of burping, farting, semi-maniacs? He was pretty sure Lizbet suspected his deception.

After Eamon explained the task, James sat down on the ground in front of the now restless gnomes and tried to explain to them about informed consent and needing to have their agreement to administer the potion, but they didn't listen. They kept looking at the sugar he'd set down on the picnic table before joining them nearer the ground. They reached their hands out to the dark potion bottle eagerly as he handed it down the row, and each of them took a healthy swig.

Well, that's that, James thought, the world is now possessed of a set of slightly smarter gnomes for about the next week.

Eamon slapped his stick again and said, "Well then, off with ye."

The gnomes scurried off together, trailing the sound of bodily noises behind them, but they didn't trip each other or run off into the woods in four different directions following some interesting flash of light. James thought that might be a good sign.

Eamon sighed. "Well, that's for it, then. Nothing to do but hope that if there's something to find, they'll find it."

James nodded, but he added his own silent wish that the little guys would be okay.

~~*

"Avenall? My name is Johnny Johnson, reporter for WGGG TV in New York. Would it be okay if I came up with my camera man and asked you a few questions?"

Avenall looked down the stairs to the man who looked up at him expectantly. "What is it you wish to speak about?"

"People are curious about you. They saw you on the news last night after passengers here emailed in their video. Do you know what a newscast is?"

"Yes, I watched many human TV shows when we still lived within the shadow realm. I understand."

"I want to put you on the news so that people can learn about you. They'd also like a closer look at your dragons."

"No one is to get close to the dragons. The younger ones are easily frightened."

"We don't need to get close. The camera can take close pictures from a distance. But we would need to come up the stairs, if that's okay."

Avenall stood for a moment, deciding. If humans understood that the dragons are not dangerous by their nature, they would be more accepting. He knew what human myth made of dragons, and they portrayed them as terrible things.

Yes, it would help to let the humans know that dragons are not meant to be beasts of destruction and war. Avenall nodded and motioned for the reporter to come forward.

"Fantastic, thank you. Why don't we set up over here by the pool, with the dragons in the background. Let's get a couple of these deck chairs and a table, maybe something to drink?"

"Captain Collins has been kind enough to provide a barrel of water. There are a number of cups. I will share with you, if you are thirsty."

The reporter walked to the water keg and placed a glass under the tap. "I was thinking of something stronger, but when in Rome..." When the glass was full, he took a long swig of the cold water and then turned to Avenall, his eyes only briefly darting to the dragons beyond so that he didn't give his true audience-grabbing interest away. He sat down in one of the deck chairs and waved his hand toward the one across from it for Avenall. "Get comfortable, and let's begin."

James and Lizbet shared a pillow on the couch where they lay snuggled up together watching television. Tanji sprawled across both arms of the big padded chair beside it.

When a promo for the nightly news started, Lizbet got up and went toward the kitchen, "Either of you want some hot chocolate?"

"Sure, thanks," said James. "Whoa, wait up. Look at that. Is he an elf?"

"Yep, he is...and wow! Those are dragons in the background. What's an elf doing on a cruise ship?"

"What's an elf doing on TV? They hate our technology and try to stay as far away from it as possible."

Tanji broke in then, suddenly sitting up straight and primping, "Guys, the important question here is—where has he been all my life? Oh my my, he is one sweet-looking elf-boy. And right there, did he say he's coming to see the queen?" She winked at Lizbet. "You lucky girl."

Lizbet shushed her so she could hear the TV. When the spot ended, Lizbet replied, "Tanj, seriously? You only broke up with Thomas like five minutes ago. Get a grip!" One eyebrow raised minutely as she continued. "Did either of you catch what he's wearing around his neck? It's a dragon claw, the insignia of a dragon tender. The elves would never let him out of the compound he's from, much less let him go on TV. She tapped the side of her head. "Morgan's going crazy in here! You'd think it was the end time instead of a few dragons."

James grabbed her without any warning indicators and pulled her close, smothering her with a huge kiss. He'd moved so quickly that the matching medallions that held the memories of their past lives came together with a metallic clank. The kiss surprised her, but she liked it and returned it.

Tanji stood abruptly and flounced into the kitchen. "Goll-ee, people! Not in front of the kids."

When Tanji was gone and James gave her her mouth back, she asked, "So what was that for?"

"I just wanted Tanji to decide to leave for a minute. Not that it wasn't fun. But you know the legends about dragon tenders, right?" James asked.

"Uh, sure...what fae queen worth her crown doesn't?"

"Thing is, they're true, according to Myrddin's memories. Some dragon tenders can speak to others and influence them with their minds."

"What? I thought there was no fae magic for mind-reading."

"It's not mind-reading. Not really. But they can communicate with other fae and humans the same way they do with dragons—they send a thought and can receive a thought back. It's not mind-reading because it's limited to thoughts the other creature is willing to share." James stopped talking for a moment, collecting the next thought from his past life treasury. "But more importantly, the very strong ones can influence people. They can force them to do things. The elves killed those stories whenever they started because of what could happen if a dragon tender discovered a talent for mind-control. That's some power there. That's why Elves with the ability to communicate with beasts are prohibited from trying to access the minds of people. If they're even suspected of trying to invade the mind of another fae, they're put to death quietly by their local council. Pretty much, dragon tenders are kept at the bottom of society so that they'll obey the elders without question. It usually works. But Myrddin has memories of one who went rogue and had a lot of fun until they caught him."

"So, you think this guy can make other people do things?"

"Yeah. I just saw him do it. Didn't you see off to the side where a guy with a camera was walking closer to the dragons, and the elf turned and looked at him, then the guy just turned around and walked away with this blank expression on his face? He can push people. Plus, he has a bunch of dragons with him. So, already a potentially dangerous guy. You need to find out what's going on with him as soon as you can. Like tonight."

"Well then, say hello to my heavy sigh, and say goodbye to Lizbet. I planned to have one Saturday night where we just got to hang out together, and I didn't have to go running around all over the world keeping track of the fae. Eamon and I weren't going to go out looking until tomorrow. I want to stay here with you guys tonight until my mom throws you out. I never get to be just me anymore! But one last thing, did you notice..." She stopped talking, not wanting to put her impression into words, sure it was just wishful thinking.

"...that kid has a strong resemblance to..." James supplied.

"Yep. Arthur—right?" Lizbet saw in his eyes the answer was yes.

"Glad it wasn't just me," he said. "Tanji didn't seem to notice, though."

"Langoureth didn't know Arthur when he was young, only when he was older and beardier and more beat up from battle. That's probably why Tanji didn't catch it."

"Just don't say anything yet about who he is if you feel like it's true once you meet him."

"Why?"

James's expression was suddenly serious as his eyes moved to hold hers. His hands moved to the ancient medallion that hung around his neck. They cupped the unfeeling metal that had brought his past life into this one as he asked, "Has knowing who you are made your life any easier or made you any happier?"

Lizbet froze, feeling guilty again about how James got stuck with a bunch of memories and history he never asked for, then she gave him a sad smile instead of an answer. She called out a goodbye to Tanji, who was still going through cupboards noisily in the kitchen, and quickly aethered away.

CHAPTER THIRTEEN

Smiling Faces Sometimes

" THE DRAGONS ARE NOBLE creatures. They aren't machines of war—it's my people who've trained them to be weapons. They're intelligent, and the herd takes care of its members in the same way that elf and human families do."

"Sure, that's interesting," the reporter said, "but let's stay with the question I asked—what about the incident in France when they attacked that guy and burned him so badly?"

"He shouted and threw stones at them. They thought they were being attacked. Any creature defends itself against attack."

"But he was just trying to get them to look his way for a picture."

Avenall patiently explained, "They are *dragons*. They do not reason as fae and humans do. They simply react."

"But just a moment ago, you said they're intelligent."

"Yes, and they deserve respect. But they are beasts all the same." Avenall tired of the man's refusal to understand. "I could leave you alone with them now, if you like, to demonstrate. You would be completely safe as long as you didn't threaten them in any way." He stood as if to leave.

The other man looked suddenly less composed. "No, I'm good." He signaled to the cameraman. "Maybe just a couple of pictures of you with the dragons to wrap up?"

"Certainly. As long as you promise not to shout or throw stones."

Johnny Johnson smiled and made a mental note; humans aren't the only race that understands sarcasm.

Afterward, Avenall felt unsettled. He should not have given in to his temper that way. But the reporter had stirred bad memories. There had been something hungry and dishonest in his eyes. Avenall thought Johnny would fit in well among the sons of Bacchus. His hand went to the dragon claw around his neck as his thoughts turned back to the sad days the reporter had forced him to recall.

Durian had tried to hold the dragon back as the man shouted, waved his arms, and tossed stones toward her, but Harul was terrified. He'd been unable to calm her. Avenall didn't tell the reporter that the dragon tender had lost his post because of the incident and that he, Avenall, had replaced his master. Nor did he wish to explain that the council didn't care that a human had been injured. They cared only that their dragon tender might not be able to keep the dragons focused on the commands of the dragon riders in battle. He was sent to tend the horses, pigs, and dogs.

After his disgrace, Durian left to live alone, deep in the forest. It is not the elven way to be so alone. Avenall had long hoped he would return. He eventually gave up that hope.

Avenall stood looking out across the ocean in the fading light of the setting sun. Just before he turned to finally rest for a while on his small cot, a movement among the waves caught his eye. What was it? A fish? No, it didn't have the silver glint of scales. It was mist, moving rapidly and keeping a discrete form, unmistlike. Not mist, then. A wisp. And there—he saw more movement just beyond.

He quickly scanned the surface of the water in the dying light. There were more. There were at least a score of them. And all of them were moving in the same direction as the ship, toward the American continent. But wisps prefer spaces near humans. Why would they travel the ocean?

"Och, do you remember the time I pulled that prank on young Molly? Sneakin' up on her like, glamoured up to be a fox?"

"Aye, I do, Hamish…" Eamon laughed as he stood to throw another log on the campfire, "What a kickin' you got that night! I never would've thought a sweet-tempered heifer like Molly could get so angry."

"She forgave me, though, over time, dinnae ye think?" Hamish asked, then spooked when Lizbet abruptly appeared from out of the aether a few feet from where he sat. Eamon had gotten used to his queen suddenly materializing from nowhere over a period of over a thousand years. Hamish was not as experienced with the ways of the auraes: his reflexive move backward toppled him off the stone where he sat. He sprawled ungracefully on his back.

"Sorry Hamish, I didn't mean to frighten you." Lizbet hid her smirk as she offered him a hand up.

Hamish was up and brushing himself off quickly, bowing low. "Dinnae concern yourself. Nothing harmed but my pride, and that was small to begin with."

"Well, I'm glad you're okay. And I'm sorry to break up your reunion, but I'm going to have to take Eamon away with me tonight. We just got an extra stop on our tour."

"How so?" Eamon asked, standing and shouldering his bag in preparation for their departure.

"There's an elf on a cruise ship heading for the US. He's apparently coming to see me, according to the news report. And he's got a herd of dragons with him. I mean, really? When he gets here, where's he going to put a herd of dragons? Anyway...it's probably better if I just go to meet him now. With everything that's going on in Europe, I don't want to wait around for surprises."

Eamon made his goodbye to Hamish and urged him to go to James if he needed anything in Eamon's absence. Then Lizbet threw a handful of pixie dust above his head, took his hand, and they were gone.

Captain Collins looked out of one of the bridge's rear windows to the stern of the ship. The security guards posted at the foot of the stairs were doing their job well. He could see the young elf lit up by the deck lights, guarding his charges as the dragons slept. He'd offered the boy an empty first class cabin, but he'd accepted only a cot and bedding and had barely used them.

He wondered if the youngster had any idea of the stir he and his dragons made by landing on the ship. He seemed to understand that the cameras pointed at him recorded his every move, but he didn't seem to understand their power. And those cameras loved him—he was handsome, composed, and polite. His spoke careful English with a strange, melodic accent. The only time his composure broke was when he was concerned about his dragons. He seemed attuned to their movements, even when his back was to them.

Whatever else it was, the dragons landing on his ship was a publicity-maker. The marketing department couldn't have come up with anything more effective. All eyes were on the ship now.

It couldn't get any better than this for his career.

And then it did.

A pretty girl with long red hair materialized on the deck with a short, ugly fae in tow. The elf went to one knee and bowed his head deeply as she started up the stairs toward him. Even from a distance, it didn't take long to figure out who the visitor was.

And now we're visited by a queen. Man, I hope I convinced the kid to stay the course. Captain Collins thought. *If he does, I can ride this one all the way to the captaincy of the best ship in the line.*

CHAPTER FOURTEEN

I'll Never Forget Your Face

WHEN THEY MATERIALIZED ON the ship, Lizbet said quietly to Eamon, "When you meet the guy, don't say anything about who he looks like, okay?"

"What do you mean?"

"Just don't," she answered sternly, as she continued up the stairs toward the pool deck.

Eamon said, "Right. No need to get testy." When he reached the top of the stairs and could see the deck beyond, he added, "Och, Would you look at those dragons? Not somethin' I'd like to meet in a dark alley, I can tell you that."

Lizbet continued walking briskly toward the young elf who awaited her on one knee on the landing. She knew there were cameras on board, and she didn't want to look hesitant when she approached him. She whispered out of the side of her mouth, "Sheesh, Eamon, you act like you've never seen a dragon before."

"Aye, I've seen one. But not this close. Never this close. I'm not a fool."

When she reached the top step and stood before the elf, he remained on one knee. She knelt down, too, and said, "Look, get up. Seriously. I hate that stuff. And call me Lizbet, okay?"

He stood up, but he kept his head bowed slightly. "As you say. I dedicate my service to you, Lizbet," He looked up and inclined his head toward the dozing dragons, "and the service of the dragons, my queen, if you pledge that you will treat them respectfully."

"I'm like the last one to be dissin' on a dragon. So, look, stand up if you want to talk to me—and you should probably introduce yourself." Lizbet held out her hand to shake. He took her hand in his. "On the news they said your name is Avenall, is that right? And this is Eamon, my bodyguard for this trip."

After shaking Lizbet's hand, Avenall bent down and stretched out his hand to Eamon, who shook it, but not without his eyebrows arching up in surprised recognition when he looked into the elf's familiar face. He recovered his composure quickly. "So, right, watch your p's and q's, laddie. I've got my eye on you."

"Is it safe to move closer to the dragons? I'd like to be out of sight of the cameras, and it seems like the only place to do that is around back of the chimney, close to where they're perched."

"Yes, it will be safe. The dragons have been calm since we landed here. They are well fed from the sea. They are content."

"Okay, then. I like a happy dragon!" She walked behind

the chimney stack and out of sight of the cameras, followed by Avenall and Eamon.

When they'd all seated themselves in deck chairs, Lizbet looked directly at Avenall, keeping her eyes fixed on his, looking for any hint of dishonesty, and asked, "Why did you leave your compound to come see me?"

He kept his eyes on hers and replied, "Because I promised Oriane I would find you and..."

Lizbet broke in, "Wait a minute. Oriane of the French fae court? The dryad?"

"Yes, that is my friend Oriane."

"So, you're *that* Avenall. She's talked about you. You're a very unusual elf. She loves you like a son."

Avenall's composure broke for a moment, and his face showed his upset. *A son—she thinks of me like a son?* Then he took back composure from the upset and said, "Yes. I am, as you say, *that* Avenall."

"If she sent you, I know I can trust you." She didn't add that Morgan's memories were nearly screaming for her to go to him, throw her arms around his neck, and tell him how she'd missed him. "So, tell me, is Oriane all right? We've been to the French court, and everyone is gone."

"I believe she is. She went to the far woods, and a dryad can hide easily in the woods if she wishes not to be found."

"Good. I'm relieved to hear that. Why did she send you?"

"Because I know where Euphemia—the one you call Mona—is. She's in grave danger, but Oriane believes she can be saved if you have a healer powerful enough."

"Mona? Fantastic!" Then the rest of what he'd said hit her. She felt a tug in her chest. "What do you mean by her needing to be saved?"

"She stands in the forest with an arrow through her heart. If she returns to her flesh form, she will die from loss of blood. However, if she remains much longer in her nature form, she will harden into a thing of the forest. There is still at least a fortnight before she is lost. Oriane made this map for you to follow." Avenall removed the map from the hidden pocket inside his tunic and handed it to her.

Lizbet opened the map and moved from the chair to the deck to spread it out in front of her. The drawing didn't look like any map she'd ever seen. It might represent trees and the forest floor, but it wasn't a very good sketch if that's what it was supposed to be. After she studied it for a while, she looked up and said, "I don't get it. How are we supposed to understand this? It doesn't look like a map to me. I don't see how we'll find Mona from this."

"It's a picture of what Euph...Mona would see around her. I fear it makes sense to a dryad because of the way they view the forest but not to a human or an elf." He sounded so sad. "I hoped you'd understand it because you are also a nymph. Perhaps I've failed my friend, after all."

Lizbet noted the wave of sadness that crossed his face. "No, I don't think so. This will help. I mean, like a lot. Maybe not so much the map, but we know now that we aren't looking for a person, we're looking for a tree. And we know what kind of help she's going to need when we find her. So, yes, it is kind of a lot of help. And maybe I can figure out this map. Or someone else can."

"With your leave, if you've not found her by the time I arrive, Fein and I could fly over the forest with your map. Fein has sharp sight, and the dryads are unique trees. They don't look like any other species."

"In what way?"

"One dryad might take the coloring and the bark of the pine but the leaves of an oak. Another might take the leaves and fruit of the chestnut but the limbs of a larch. It is unique to each dryad. I do not know which characteristics your Mona has when she joins with nature, but I am well acquainted with many trees and would be able to tell if I had found one that does not exist in the forest."

"Okay. You're on the team. When will you be able to get to Ohio?"

"The dragons are rested now. We'll take flight again and should arrive within the span of eight days. It will be difficult because the dragons will need some place to rest. The captain tells me that there are other ships that travel these waters at this season, but only a very few. It is my hope to find them. We have not yet tried resting upon the sea."

"It's too bad the dragons are too big for me to pull you all through the aether. If Aisha was here, it wouldn't be a problem. That chick has some serious skills. But I could maybe take you and one of the small ones, and Eamon could take the long way with the rest of them. Not that I know what we're going to do with them when you get there."

At this, Eamon, who'd been only half listening as he kept one eye on the dragons, sprang alert. "I'll be no part of a plan that has me shepherding dragons. T'isn't going to happen. Can't they just travel all the way by boat? This one seems to be going at a good clip. When's it supposed to arrive?"

"We will be in a country called Florida within the next three days, yet I am not at ease here with all of these people near the dragons. And if we stay with this ship, we would still have another two long days of flight to your land of Ohio. The captain has shown me a map and given me this." Avenall held up a compass.

"All right, it's settled then. I'm your queen, and I say you stay on the boat because that's what makes sense. You'll be in Ohio, like, three days earlier? Hopefully we'll have found Mona by then and your help won't be needed... although, don't you want to go home now that you've delivered Oriane's message?"

"No. I can never return. I've committed treason. Nor will I allow my people to ruin these dragons by training them to be forces of destruction." Avenall's green eyes flashed anger, and the dragons stirred behind him. Avenall took a deep breath and lowered his head, then raised it again, fully calm. The dragons settled back in. "I am ashamed of my people. Ashamed of what they have done and what they have not yet done. I know they've captured many of the dryads, and I know they've killed a human who was outside the gates."

"Do you know why they did that?"

"I no longer know why they do anything. From the day you rescued us from the shadow realm, it has been as if the elves have lost their minds and their honor—all of them, all at once. It was terrible in the shadow realm, but they have never joyed in being released from it."

"They'd have to have gone crazy if they expect they can just get all of the humans out of the way at once. I mean, there's a lot of us around. Is that really what they think?"

"Yes. But I don't know why they think it. It seems unreasonable to me. Nor would I wish to see that happen. That is why I took the dragons and have come to serve you."

"Okay, I get that, but here's how it is: I don't know what I'm supposed to do with you. There's no North American court where you can stay. The fae native to my country have never been organized like the European fae were, and they aren't interested in the politics. Plus, there are plenty of wide open places out west where they can still be left alone, even if those places are pretty barren. But I guess I'll figure something out."

Lizbet took his hand and held it for a while between both of hers. Inside her, where Morgan's memories lived, her past life called to his, and she felt so much joy in the touch. She didn't want to let him go but knew she had to. She dropped his hand and said, "Okay, I need to get going now. I've got fae to find."

She released his hand, then turned and took Eamon's as she flung a handful of dust into the air. As they disappeared, she muttered, "Dragons. Sheesh. Where am I going to put a bunch of dragons?"

CHAPTER FIFTEEN
Going Underground

EAMON TUGGED HIS HAND away from Lizbet's grasp on a narrow balcony near the top of the fae castle in Spain. It was late and they wouldn't be able to enjoy the view from the top of the mountain where the stone castle snuggled into the cliffs. They stood there quietly for a moment, waiting for sounds of activity within. In the courtyard below, there was only silence and shadow.

"Seems deserted here, but let's go see what we can see," Lizbet said finally.

They entered the turret through a thick wooden door. They walked carefully down the worn stone steps that were lit only by the moonlight in the open sky above them. They exited on the ground floor, where they would normally be greeted by at least one or two of the resident fae who sensed their arrival on the "landing pad" above. No one greeted them this time.

Lizbet eased the backpack off her shoulders and again took out a plastic bag full of roughly ground leaves which she held close to her mouth and whispered into, then blew off of her palm. The starweed gathered at the ceiling, illuminating the room.

"Well, lassie, I see you've added to your bag of tricks."

"Yep, I've been working on it. But I'd rather be studying physics or be out riding my bike than sitting alone with Morgan's memories studying up on my magic. At least James and Tanji help me out with some of it once in a while, so I'm not so bored. Do you think I'm just too rational to be a sorceress?"

Eamon smiled to himself, thinking of the laughing girl falling in the mud over and over as she learned how to use her wings. "Distracted by other things for now, perhaps. But too rational for magic? Nay, I think not."

It was too quiet in the castle, Lizbet knew, as she and her companion went from chamber to chamber looking for the fae and finding no one. Just as at the Scottish court and the fortress of the nymphs in Greece, it was empty. There was no clue left behind to help them learn what had happened to the inhabitants.

"I don't know, Eamon. I don't know what to do. They can't all just be gone."

"Aye, I agree. But as to what happened, I have no more idea than you."

"Well, we can't just keep going from site to site finding nothing. I say we stay here tonight since all the beds are still made up. Then we can take a look around tomorrow to see if we can find anything to point to what happened."

"It's a good plan. But I'll not sleep. Choose your chamber, and I'll make myself comfortable just outside of it."

Lizbet bent down slightly to grab his hand and gave it a squeeze. "I couldn't ask for a better friend than you."

"Och, it's nothin', it's my duty to my queen." He brushed her hand away, looking flustered.

"Sure. Whatever," Lizbet said, grinning.

～～*

"Are you sure you've had enough biscuits, Eamon?" Louis, Sr. asked as he offered the plate heaped with a variety of cookies. Eamon approved of the fare provided by his cab-driving friend in London much more than the bologna sandwiches and apples they'd had at the Spanish court the night before. Lizbet's mother had packed plenty of hot chocolate and sugar, but she hadn't planned the bagged lunches carefully enough for his liking. Unfortunately, the castle's kitchens had also been cleared of the treats that were usually stored there.

Eamon held up a hand as if to decline, but then said, "Well, there does seem to be a surplus I might help with," as he scooped up another handful of shortbread and chocolate discs. "Thank ye, Louis, for the hospitality, as always."

"It's a bribe, mate, I want to know what's happening in the land of the fae. It's dull here with James gone home." He turned to Lizbet, who sat next to Eamon on the worn but comfortable couch. "Lizbet? Another bickie?"

"I'm good," she said over the rim of her tea cup, "But you do have a little guy over there who's been waiting patiently for his turn at the plate." She inclined her head toward Louis, Jr., who sat on the floor at the edge of the coffee table, his huge brown eyes following the platter of treats.

Louis, Sr. faked surprise and said, "Louis, I'd completely forgotten about you. You wouldn't want another biscuit, would you? And spoil your dinner?"

Little Louis's eyes grew wider at this but before he could speak up to say that he very much did want another biscuit, his father's booming laugh filled the room and he set the entire plate of cookies before his son, saying, "see that you keep an eye on that."

The boy happily dipped his newfound riches into his glass of milk and delivered them into his mouth one after another, but whenever Lizbet looked in his direction as the adults talked she could see he absorbed every word as surely as the cookies absorbed the milk.

"So, we've been to the Scottish court, the Spanish court, and the nymph's fortress. We also went to a few of the centaur villages in Europe, and they're all deserted. It's like people just dropped what they were doing and disappeared. The elves are still in their compounds, though. So, hey, no problem there."

"Do you think the elves did something to them? I know you were talking about rumors of war the last time you stopped in, but I didn't think there were enough elves to take on all of the other magical folk."

"There are upwards of eighty thousands elves in the known encampments. Plus, there has always been talk of unmapped fortresses where the most conservative of the elves have themselves hidden. But even then, there would be what? At the most, like a hundred thousand elves and another twenty thousand followers among the other fae? That would be who? Maybe the spriggans, and the other "wild folk" Avenall mentioned, and there is apparently a reason to believe the sons of Bacchus are involved—James only just filled me in on who they are. I didn't think the elves were a real threat. I thought they'd be too smart to make that kind of trouble when they're so outnumbered.

"But Hamish told you the elves attacked the Scottish court?"

Eamon replied for her, "Aye, and it was a fearsome thing, he says. They captured many and killed a few. But they left it as if nothing had happened there. Much like what we've observed everywhere else. That's why we're concerned."

"It's not like they haven't acted like this before. I've been told the elves also tried to take over the rule of the fae two thousand years ago. James said they got slapped down good by the centaurs, so they pretty much gave up and tried to play nicer with everyone after that. Of course, they hadn't captured all the dragons yet, either. But even with that, I just can't see them making that many fae just disappear."

At the end of the table, Louis, Jr. stopped dipping his biscuits in milk and said, "Everybody's gone? All the people I met when you took me to the court? Even Aisha? Aisha visited us last night. She likes daddy."

The heads of both visitors swiveled abruptly to the adult Louis at the other end of the table. Lizbet raised an eyebrow in silent inquiry.

Louis, Sr. shrugged. "Apparently there's this thing the nymphs have. It's not like I encouraged her. We met when you asked us to court, remember? I was just interested in learning more. You know how curious I am about everything fae."

"What a minute—what thing nymphs have?" Lizbet asked, hoping for an answer that didn't include lifetime nymph bonding like Morgan had with Myrddin.

"Like a soulmate thing, I guess. She says despite the thousands of men she's known in her lifetime, I'm the one she's destined for. Thousands of men—that's not intimidating."

"Och, that's not good," Eamon said.

"Hey, it's not so bad. I think I feel the same way. And I've missed having someone in my life since Louis's mother died."

"But you're human, Louis. Aisha will mourn you forever when you're gone." Eamon sighed deeply.

"I hope to stick around for a while, mate." He smiled his brilliant smile.

Lizbet interrupted. "Okay, so...love lives with immortal beings out of the way—not that it's not cool and everything that you're all lovey-dovey—but do you have any idea where she might have gone?"

"None. She didn't mention anything about being in hiding. We don't talk about the fae much. Why do you think I'm dying for gossip?"

Lizbet looked exasperated.

A small voice broke in. "What about the under-courts?"

Heads swiveled again, this time in the other direction.

"From the mouth of a child! Why didn't I think of it? How do you know about those, lad?"

"Aisha told me a bedtime story about the elven war and how the nymphs hid themselves in the underground castles the fae used to have. She said they were perfect because all of the entrances were closed a long time ago and almost no one remembers where they are. Plus, you can't get to some of them except through the aether."

"You remember the story well, lad. Aye, it's a great one from our history."

"What are you guys talking about?" Lizbet asked.

"Och, that's right. The human Morgan didn't know a great deal about the history of the fae, not having been raised among them. You wouldn't necessarily know the story. I keep forgettin' how spotty your education has been. But

I think it's time to take our leave, and to do it gratefully. I'll educate you when we get there. Young Louis here may have solved a mystery."

Lizbet took a deep breath and let it back out again, shaking her head. "You know, I'll never understand why fae can't just pick up a phone and let a person know what's going on instead of leaving clues and hints and dropping little random snippets of 411."

* ～ * ～ *

When Lizbet emerged from the aether with Eamon in the cavernous space, the sheer volume of voices talking at once overwhelmed her. The high ceiling inside the mountain at the location of Dumbarton Castle bounced the sound back toward the hard stone floor beneath them. As the fae engaging in various activities around them noticed them, the voices began to fall silent. A beautiful woman with long red hair hurried forward.

"Lizbet, my sister," she exclaimed as she threw her arms around her. "You've been to see my sweet Louis, yes?"

"Yes, Aisha, I have. If I hadn't, I would never have found you."

"I would have come for you sooner or later, be sure of that. You are our queen. I simply wished to see Louis more than I wished to see you. And I have been too busy for all the days since the elves attacked to take more than just a few moments away from gathering our people."

"It's not possible for everyone to be in here."

"No, that is true. But there are other under-castles in the lands the humans call Spain and France, and also near the court in the High Lands. And more, not all of us are below ground. The forest folk who could not bear to be so enclosed—the centaurs, the few remaining free dryads—have gone deeper into the forests, as far from the elven compounds as they can roam. I or one of our sister auraes stop with each of the bands daily to be sure that nothing ill has befallen them. But now, come, we will have refreshment, and I will tell you what I know."

CHAPTER SIXTEEN
Stick To The Plan

"I DEMAND YOUR SILENCE!" Shan brought the empty palms of his hands down on the wooden table, producing a loud slap. The council quieted, turning their attention to him again.

"There is no need for this arguing among ourselves." He continued where he left off. "I tell you again that the Abomination is still alive not because our assassin has not done his job but because he has done it exceedingly well. The Abomination believes that we have accepted him among us. He believes he will return to our compound when his task is done. We could not achieve what we are planning without him. Have none of you noticed that the wisps are gone? He is gathering all of this loose magic for a spell which will wither the roots of human power. I can think of no better use for the soulless things."

"First you say the Abomination is still alive, and then

that you are working in concert with him! Have you no sense of decency?" challenged Elder Groux. The chorus of voices rose again.

"Be silent, all of you," Shan thundered. "He is but a tool. A powerful wizard when we have none of our own strong enough to counter the human machinery of war. Have you forgotten what they did to each other while we were in the shadow realm? The devastation wrought by their bombs and flying ships? Our dragons and magic are but laughable next to their power to destroy."

"But the Abomination? You have told him he can live among us!"

"Yes, the assassin Freoric has told him that. I ask you, Elder Groux—would *you* believe the word of an assassin?"

There was laughter then around the room. Groux held up his hands to quiet it.

"I see your meaning now, Shan. Can you guarantee that this Abomination will not come among us when your plan has been worked?"

"Yes. I can guarantee it. He will never set foot within this compound."

Groux nodded his head. "Then my fears are laid to rest. I will wait to judge until I have seen the outcome of this plan."

Oriane heard the lock being pulled and yanked back the root tendril that snaked from the tiny gap in the top of a boot. If she was discovered attempting communication, it would mean her death. She knew this, but she had lived long and would make an end of it gladly if it meant she could warn the humans what was coming. Her queen, Lizbet, was a human girl, and Oriane loved her dearly. Nor would she have sent Avenall to take risks she would not take herself.

The tendril shortened and disappeared before elder Shan entered the chamber. He smiled as he addressed her.

"Your plotting with the dragon tender has been undone. We now know where he has gone. When he arrives, he will be dealt with."

"What has happened to the elves, Shan? What has happened to you? Have you no affection for your own son? Have you no affection for your people?"

"I have no son!" he thundered. "My concern is *only* for my own people. You and the other fae follow a human queen. No fae, not even the most undisciplined of the wild folk, should ever place himself beneath a human."

"Do you still believe that the elves can battle the humans and win?"

"The elves are not alone in this. There are many who have thrown their power in with us. The unaligned fae, even the good folk, have joined us from their hidden homes. And soon, the humans will be stripped of the things that give them power to resist us in battle. In the end, it will be no battle at all. We will simply take from them what we want and require they leave us alone or die on our swords. It will be as it was in the days before Myrddin's truce."

"You would breach Myrddin's truce while Myrddin lives again? I am impressed, Shan. You must have no fear of death."

"I have no fear of the newborn wizard who styles himself Myrddin. As in the olden times, he has no heart for revenge. Was it not this reborn Myrddin who took his own murderer as a friend? In the old times, he never entered battle without the support of his human king, Arthur. No,

I have no fear of him. And I have a much stronger wizard at my command."

"Stronger than Myrddin? None is stronger."

"Yes. A stronger wizard has risen to champion the elves. Indeed, there are two who are stronger. And one of them is placed with the queen. Surely you remember Faolan? Faolan risen is ten times stronger than Myrddin,"

"The boy Thomas has no superior strength. He is only an apprentice."

"I think you will be surprised by the strength he has. You and the humans will choke on your surprise when all is revealed." Shan turned then. He smiled to himself with satisfaction as he left the room.

When he was gone, Oriane slowly unleashed the tendril from the opening in the boot again, bidding it grow until it bridged the gap between the bottom of her metal cage and the floor. She watched it snake toward the small crack she had found with constant probing. She pushed the tendril downward, hoping to encounter the bare earth that must be below the stone and mortar.

There, there it was. The root contacted good earth and the spark of her communication moved from bacteria to nematode to root to bacteria, tracing its way along the path of underground life toward Euphemia. She held her breath for a response and let it out when the response came.

The message from Euphemia was faint, but it gave her hope. *I'm fading, dear sister, but I'm still here.*

Avenall tried to remain patient with the slow progress across the ocean. The dragons were bored and restless. On a normal day, they would hunt and train. Their diet would be varied, comprised of game as well as fish, and their minds would be better occupied by the training routine than by perching and waiting. If he had not made a promise to the queen, he would have let them follow their instincts and continue on without the ship as a source of refuge. But he'd made a promise and he would not break it even if the dragons pushed at him to allow them their freedom.

Avenall was bored by his new routine, too. He had his music, but he had little else to occupy him. He didn't feel comfortable leaving the dragons and exploring the other areas of the ship. The captain insisted that the security personnel at the entrance to the pool deck would make sure that nothing happened to the dragons, but that was not what concerned him. The dragons could fend for themselves. It was the passengers he worried about. Many of them congregated below the pool deck, hoping for a glimpse of the herd. It only took one of them to try to get their attention in an aggressive way, and...

He knew It must have been terrible for Durian. To be inside Harul's mind as she flamed, using all of his strength to try to restrain her. And still, he had watched helplessly as the dragon's fire blazed toward the man she saw as an attacker.

Avenall thought back to the last time he saw his friend and teacher. Durian had come to him after the council was done with him—bloodied, humiliated, and sent to tend the pigs. Even a dragon tender is higher than a farmer in elven society. It was too much for the gentle man whose ways Avenall had gladly followed. When Durian quietly took his own dragon claw and placed it around Avenall's neck, he believed he understood the gesture, the passing of responsibility from master to apprentice, but it was the tears in Durian's eyes that told him it was more.

It is not the elven way to express affection between men, but Avenall clasped Durian's hands on the chain of the medallion, and their eyes meeting briefly, before he let go and watched the older man dart to the fence and slip into the forest.

The dragons stirred as fresh pain welled up unexpectedly at this memory. Avenall forced himself to send thoughts of ease and relaxation to them. He wondered how he would ever be able to do the same for himself.

Even if he could return to the elves one day, there was no one left there who cared for him. All he had now was the responsibility left around his neck by Durian of caring for the dragons. He would honor that responsibility for as long as the dragons needed him.

CHAPTER SEVENTEEN
I've Got You Under My Skin

THOMAS WATCHED THE WISP enter the silo and drape itself momentarily over the glass lip of the globe before it slipped inside and joined with the others. He didn't know how many wisps had already contributed themselves to his project, but there were more arriving every day. They slipped in a few at a time, in a slow but steady stream. At first, he was concerned the humans might notice the wisps were on the move, gliding past them silently on the way to Ohio. But what would it matter? Soon the globe would be full, and the flow of wisps would stop.

As another wisp topped the high cement wall above him in a rush toward the globe, he held out his hands to gather it to himself instead. With only a little hesitation, it slipped through his chest to join with the power he'd already captured from the others of its kind. He breathed a satisfied sigh. The blue glow that lit up his skin slowly faded as he forced the magic to move closer to his core. It was an effort, but he worked at it constantly to prevent the glow, now sometimes visible in the dark, from giving him away.

~~*

With the shop closed on Mondays, Tanji wasn't surprised to see Thomas walking toward her as she neared the woods. He greeted her with, "All right, Tanj?"

She knew his gift for sensing the magic of others allowed him to locate any of the magical folk who were close enough to his location. The range of his gift even seemed to have grown since they started dating. After the homecoming dance, he'd only been able to sense her as she drove toward his apartment from a block or two away. Anymore, he seemed to know if she left her house. That actually made for some weird moments when he'd turned up when she wasn't expecting him. He may not have been very attentive most of the time, but he could definitely be jealous.

She sighed and replied, "Oh hey, imagine seeing you here." She rolled her eyes on the inside but didn't show it on the outside.

"I sensed you," Thomas replied, to which Tanji said, "Well, duh." Or maybe she only said it on the inside. What she really wanted to do was to tell him to stop creeping on her. Really loud. On the outside.

But she just let him walk along as she went toward the small path into the woods. "You know how I told you the other day at work that Mona's missing? I thought I'd nose around a little more near where James found her shoe now that the snow's melted a little."

"Looking for clues? I could lend a hand."

"Sure, okay. You really haven't had any tingles going about Mona? You haven't felt her magic lately?"

"No, I can't say that I have. She must be out of range." He ducked ahead and held aside the branch of a bramble that crossed into the path. "I wish I could remember the last time I sensed her."

"We've all been tossing it around over and over, trying to remember any little thing that might help us find her. Lizbet's mom is going out of her head. So, I thought I'd put some more effort in. Mrs. Moore is like a second mom to me, especially since my mom has been gone so much."

"That's right—your mother's visiting, isn't she? When's she leaving?"

"She'll be here for at least another week while she makes arrangements for her move. We're having tomorrow as a mother-daughter talk day. I kind of wish I was, like, five and didn't get treated so much like an adult on this one. My dad gets it, but my mom has this bad habit of talking to me like I'm a girlfriend instead of her kid. I used to think that was cool, but now that it's going to be about her and dad's relationship, I don't think I really want to know, you know?"

"No, I don't know. I don't remember having parents." He didn't sound upset. He was just stating a fact.

Tanji suddenly remembered Thomas's lack of memories. "Sorry. I forgot about that. Well, just trust me on this one, oh-man-with-no-past."

"I'll do that." Thomas took her elbow and said, "We should try this way, I think. Didn't Mona use one of the clearings over here a lot when she contacted Europe? Didn't we walk with her here once?"

"Yeah, but I was thinking I'd start where we found her shoes."

"I thought you said you looked around there already?"

"We did, but there was snow on the ground, and it could have covered something up."

"Makes sense." He dropped her arm and followed after her. She couldn't see his look of frustration. Then he called out, "Hey, wait a minute, didn't you see this when you walked by?"

Tanji turned and looked where he was pointing. She picked the scrap of cloth off a thorny branch. "Oh wow—that's blood, isn't it? It could be hers. I don't recognize the fabric, but I don't know what she was wearing, either. Whoever it was had to be in a big hurry to tear their clothes instead of stopping to untangle them."

"Let me see," he said, taking the scrap of cloth from her. "It does have a residual feel of magic, although it's too degraded for me to say for certain it's her magical signature. And look, there are some broken branches further on. Looks like someone went this way."

"Wow, you must have eagle eyes. Let's go." Tanji hurried off along the narrow side path, in danger of tearing her own clothes among the thick brambles. She hoped she'd be bringing home good news about her lost friend.

The summons felt like a giant hand clamping around him and dragging him forward. Freoric had no choice but to follow it. By the time he reached Thomas at the concrete silo, he was mute from swallowing his rage. It infuriated him that this thing created of human and wisp should be allowed to treat him as a servant. And yet, he was following the orders of his council and serving the interests of the elves. He would bear it for a short while longer, but when this time was over...

He waited in silence until Thomas turned and spoke.

"I'm pleased with how well you laid the trail away from the dryad's location."

Freoric forced himself to speak. "It was a simple enough task for a woodsman."

"I was surprised to sense you'd drifted so far from the silo while I was with Tanji in the woods. I told you to stay close."

"I heard something. I went to investigate. I was sure you'd approve."

Thomas stepped closer to the elf and spoke quietly but intensely, "Investigate only what comes into sight. My spell will keep away any but the most determined. I explained this to you when I created the ward to protect you from the magic."

"You did. Perhaps because I cannot feel the dread myself, I've doubted it's strength. I will not doubt again."

"Or maybe you should experience it so you'll understand." Thomas held out his hand. "Remove the charm, and let me hold it for you. You'll beg to have it back."

Freoric bobbed his head in an unfamiliar gesture of obedience, wanting to hand Thomas the moving, thrusting blade of his hunting knife instead of the leather pouch he wore on a thong around his neck. He had no choice but to comply and put the charm into the other's hand, maintaining a blank expression even as the terror took hold of him body and mind. His heart raced, his bowel spasmed. He felt he was in danger of falling to his knees and begging for the charm to be returned. It was difficult to breath, but he refused to gasp for the air he so desperately needed. Nothing could betray his distress.

Thomas stood looking at him calmly for a moment. Then smiled.

"You're very strong-minded, Freoric. I admire that. Would you like the charm back?"

He replied quietly through gritted teeth. "Yes." It was all he could say with the small amount of breath he had left.

Thomas handed the charm to him. With a slow, controlled movement, Freoric returned it to hang around his neck .

Someday, it would be his great pleasure to kill this Abomination.

CHAPTER EIGHTEEN
Breakin' Up Is Hard To Do

"TANJI, ARE YOU EVEN listening?"

Tanji looked up from the plate of food she was toying with. She was sitting across from her mother in the dining room of the town's best—but still not very good—hotel. "Sorry. I've got a lot on my mind. I may have found some more information about what happened to a friend who disappeared, and I texted it to James. He's going to go out and look again when he gets home from work. I'm just worried that with more time going by, the chance of finding her gets less and less."

"What friend?"

"She's a half-fae like me, named Mona. She works for Dad, so she's not a kid. I sometimes tease her and call her 'Mona the Telephona'. She puts up with me, so..."

"Yes, I've heard of Mona from your father. He speaks highly of her. I'm sure what you found will help, toonkins.

But I need you to pay attention to what I'm sayin' to you now. I want us to have only honesty between us. I want to make sure you don't blame your father for anything that's happened."

"Why would I blame him? Did he do something wrong? I can't imagine him doing anything to hurt you."

"He would never hurt me. But I've hurt him by letting things go on so long. I wanted us to make it for you. We both love you so much, but that isn't enough when two people can never be right together."

"What? You and dad have always gotten along great!"

"Yes, we're very good friends. He's my best friend. But I have dreams, Tanji-girl, and they're starting to come true for me in the city. Your father and I have never agreed on the kind of life we wanted to lead."

Tanji stopped eating mid-bite. "So, you just decide to take off and leave him because he'd rather build houses for gnomes than dress up in a suit and make money for stockholders?"

Her mother gave her a patient look. "I did try to make it work. We'd agreed to stay together until you graduated from high school, but..."

"Yeah, yeah, he'd be understanding. That's my daddio. But wow—you guys couldn't just come clean and tell me instead of drawing it out for the past year? Like I'm stupid and didn't get that you living in New York almost all the time wasn't normal?"

"Please don't be like that. We just...neither of us was in a hurry, that's all. We're still friends, and it isn't easy to end a marriage. But now I'm in a hurry. I've been offered an amazing opportunity, and I can't pass it up. It won't leave me time to run back to Ohio to pretend that everything is the same as it's always been. There's a lot of travel. It just seemed like the right time to tell you."

"Yeah, I mean—mom, I get it, and I'm not mad at you, really. You're mi madre, comprende? It's just going to take a while for me to get my head around it. Plus, I can't believe that you and dad were like constantly saying 'always be honest with yourself and other people', and for the whole past year or so, you've been lying to me!"

"Yes." Her mother leaned across the table to place her hand on Tanji's cheek. "Yes, and it was wrong of us. Your father wanted to tell you, but I begged him to give you a little more time to be our little girl."

When her mother removed her hand, Tanji felt like she was going to start crying again and gave a small laugh instead to cover. "Well, no biggie. I mean, I might as well be a 'child of divorce' along with everything else. It's not like life is turning out exactly the way I thought it would anyway."

Tanji slipped onto the couch where her father sat reading after stopping at the fridge for a bowl of ice cream. She stretched out to lounge over one of the puffy arms and picked up the remote. She surfed through the channels but couldn't find anything to stick with, so she flipped through her choices over and over again.

Her father interrupted the fourth round of channel roulette. "I guess that's the end of my quiet time, then?"

"Sorry. I can go upstairs and watch."

"No need." He put his book down on the end table. "James told me on the way back from a pixie capture that you found some new information about Mona?"

"Yeah, maybe. At least I hope so. Was he going out to look for her?"

"He said he was. From what I know of James, if he says he's going to do something, he does it."

"Yeah, he does. Lizbet definitely lucked out when the universe picked her soulmate."

"I hope Mona turns up soon. I miss her."

"Yeah." Tanji nodded halfheartedly, distracted.

"So, since you're obviously not volunteering anything, how was dinner with your mother?"

"It was fine." Tanji stabbed at the ice cream with her spoon. "You guys didn't need to stay together for me if you were unhappy. I mean, I wish she wasn't going to New York, but I wouldn't make her stay here just to make me happy."

"No. Neither would I," he said, as the glimmer of a tear appeared in the corner of his eye. He blinked it away.

"Oh dad..."

"Sweetheart, it's okay. We don't need to talk about how I feel, because you don't need to deal with the part that isn't about how much both your mother and I love you. You get that, right?"

"Whatevs. Now we're both single."

"You're still sure about the breakup with Thomas?"

"Yeah, it's kind of like what mom said. That sometimes people just don't want the same things." Her father flinched a little at this, but Tanji was looking off, remembering the conversation, and didn't see it. "I mean, I think about Thomas, and I still think he is one hot guy, plus crazy smart, and for a while he really started to loosen up and be fun. Then about a month ago, he went weird. Like, gonzo weird even for Thomas."

"No offense, but that's pretty weird."

"I know, right? He's gotten secretive and he acts like

he barely knows I'm there most of the time. He's always someplace else in his head. And when I want to hang out, he's like 'I can't, I've got this thing I have to do', but he can't ever say what it is. Says that he'll tell me 'in the fullness of time'. Really, he said that—'in the fullness of time'—and that I will really like it. So what can that be about?"

Ron made a ya-got-me gesture . "So, how long will it take you to add 'in the fullness of time' to your favorite phrases list?"

"So kill me. I like words! Anyway, I get it now—what maybe you tried to tell me when I first asked if we could go out—we're two people who aren't right for each other."

"I always thought so, and it wasn't about the age difference. I just didn't see how the two of you were going to mesh. Even as friends, you don't have much in common."

"Well, thanks for letting me waste a couple of months of my dating life on a freak." Tanji stuck her tongue out at him, then turned serious. "I do mean that—about letting me figure it out on my own. I just wish Thomas would get a clue. He acts like we're still dating. And we are soooo not dating."

Freoric picked up the cage and tipped it sideways, shaking it to force the pixie dust off the bottom and into the ceramic bowl below. Inside the cage, the angry pixie buzzed and tried to bite his fingers through his heavy leather gloves. Freoric ignored the creature and set the cage back down harshly, sending the pixie slamming against the bars. It let out a pained yelp and then whimpered softly as Freoric picked up the bowl and walked away.

It was the darkest hour of the night. He had no fear of

being discovered as he passed along what Thomas had told him the day before.

He removed a roll of blank manuscript from his pouch, sliced a section off, and returned the rest to its hiding place. With a quill dipped in a small inkwell, writing as much by feel as by sight in the dim moonlight, he scratched out the message he'd been waiting to send.

He wrote the details: *it is almost done.* He didn't write of his anticipation of the end of the plan, of his excitement about completing the job he'd been sent to London to accomplish before following Thomas to this far land. But he felt the excitement and anticipation keenly.

When he was done, he folded the packet, placed it into a small wooden box and shook the pixie dust into it. He put the lid back on and recited the words he'd been taught.

When he next opened the lid, the message was gone.

Chapter Nineteen
We Sail The Ocean Blue

AVENALL SAT STIFFLY AT the table, unsure what to do with some of the utensils around his plate of food. The knife and the spoons were familiar. The implements with short prongs were more of a mystery. They would not be found on an elven table. And why did he need two? He watched the other diners long enough to determine these tools were used to skewer the food just as a knife would be used. He picked one up to begin his meal. It served its purpose admirably.

That he had landed on a ship full of human elders and their mates was clear by the abundance of servants to bring them their food and drink, clear their dishes, and make sure that their needs were met. He was uncomfortable among the passengers despite his father's place in elven society. He preferred the easy comfort of the barn and its inhabitants, but he could not say no to the captain every time he was asked for his presence. He would appear ungrateful. He'd felt obligated to accept the kind man's hospitality.

Seated on either side of him were pretty young women dressed in rich fabrics. Their bodies were more exposed than he was used to. They giggled and flattered him, making his face redden. He had little experience of females and had too recently learned that the one he cared for most thought of him as a son, a feeling that would forever prevent her from seeing him the way he wished she would see him.

He was glad when the silver-haired woman across the table addressed him.

"If you don't mind me asking, what was it like living in the shadow realm? I've never really understood what people mean by that when they talk about where the fae were before Fae Day."

How could he describe the shadow realm to someone who had never experienced it? It was a long moment before he answered. "On your TV, I've seen stories about ghosts who walk the world. In the shadow realm, we were like ghosts of your world and only real in ours. We had no reality except what was invested with magic. There was little food, and little drink. We starved from morning till night with only the magic of the Tree of Life sustaining us."

The heavy man at the woman's left stopped eating to say, "I don't believe it. No one could live like that. You're what, sixteen or seventeen years old? How could you grow up without food?" He started rhythmically shoveling his meal into his mouth again, but he continued looking at Avenall, his eyes demanding an answer.

"As I said, we starved, but we did not die. Those who wished to die without an act of violence had to state their desire to the Tree or it would go on sustaining them for their natural lifetimes. Some chose this path to the other side. My father told me my own mother ended her life this way and walked into the forest to die of exposure once her request was granted."

The silver-haired woman reached across the table and patted his hand gently, "Oh dear, that's so sad. I didn't mean to upset you. I just want to understand the fae better."

The man next to her stopped wolfing his dinner again to inject, "I don't believe a word of it. I think the fae are just playing us all for sympathy."

Avenall didn't have time to respond. The captain was standing now at the head of the table and addressed him. "Avenall, if you've finished eating, I'd enjoy your company on a walk around the deck."

Glad to be rescued from the uncomfortable situation, Avenall was quick to bid his dinner partners goodbye. He was sure many fae would try to trick humans, but even so, the humans had no understanding that a good number of the fae blamed them for their captivity in the shadow realm. It had been, after all, a human who took everything away from the fae at a time when the races had been most at peace.

As he fell into step beside the captain, the captain said, "I'm sorry about what that passenger said. I should have chosen our dinner partners more carefully. It seems I mostly got it wrong. I didn't mean for you to be uncomfortable."

"If I am to be among humans, perhaps it is better not to be protected from what they believe. I find humans are much like elves despite their greater freedom to choose their own paths."

"What you described—surviving without food, drink, the basics of survival. That's how you lived?"

"Yes. But I grew up with privilege until my magic manifested, and we had a share of whatever was available. Plants and creatures invested with magic were solid in our realm and could be consumed, but there was not enough to go around. My father is an important man in our society. Eldest of an influential council of elders. In our culture, "elder" no longer refers to age, although it once did. He is still a young man in a position that can be obtained through battle, influence, or wealth." He didn't add that his father purchased his position and may have poisoned his way to the top after that. It is what the servants said, anyway, when no one thought their master's son was within hearing distance.

Captain Collins took his leave at the base of the pool deck stairs. "I think I'll miss you when you're gone. I'll always be happy to find a berth for you if you want to travel with us again."

As he watched the captain walk away, Avenall felt sure he would never again travel the sea again, although he was glad of his new friend's invitation. He would not leave the dragons. They were now the only family he had, and a ship was no home for them.

Avenall woke early as the gray light of false dawn lit the darkness. The dragons were restless. He could feel Fein pushing at his mind. He opened himself. Through Fein's eyes, he saw the tiniest glimpse of land on the horizon. They were nearly to the queen's land. It was time for them to depart.

He gave the dragons leave to fish and feed while he went himself to the large open room where humans congregated for their meals. He filled a rough cloth bag with enough bread, cheese, and canned liquids to keep himself fed for the rest of his journey. If he was right, they could make it to the queen's village in two long days of flight. Avenall felt secure the dragons could do this. They were thoroughly rested and fed now, and it would be no hardship for them in this condition.

Avenall returned to the upper deck and lashed his store of food into the larger pack he strapped securely to the pommel of his saddle. He unpacked the extra furs he would need to wear for warmth as they traveled farther north, then walked across the deck to visit the captain where he commanded the ship.

When Captain Collins saw Avenall peering through the bridge windows, he smiled, then walked to the door and onto the deck to greet the young elf. "Morning. How'd you sleep?"

"I am well rested, thank you. But the dragons can see the land now, and they are eager to return to flight. I would not hold them longer, but I will miss your hospitality and friendship."

"And I'll miss you, too, kid. Are you sure you can't stay until we disembark? There are a lot of people on shore who'd be pleased to meet you."

"No, I have a purpose in this trip. And it's time to continue it the way we started."

The captain offered his hand. "It's goodbye, then. Have a safe trip. And good luck."

Collins watched the elf walk away. He truly liked the kid—who wouldn't? But that was one heck of a meal ticket he was letting escape. His ship was going to be less interesting to the media from now on, even if he could manage a few perks due to the interviews he already had lined up.

The media had started calling this trip "The Dragon Cruise", and he wasn't going to disappoint anyone by telling tame tales of dragons lazing around on the pool deck and fishing off the stern. He was already working up something much more interesting from Avenall's stories of his father and his experiences in the shadow realm. People didn't need to hear how calm the dragons had been. Dragons aren't always calm. Stretching the truth a little never hurt anybody.

CHAPTER TWENTY

Up In The Air, Junior Birdman

IN THE CAFETERIA, TANJI sat down and shoved her phone into Lizbet's hand before opening her pack and pulling out the lunch bag which contained her daily regimen of magic-enhancing foods. She said, "There's your boy. Looks like he left the ship and was last reported flying the friendly skies over West Virginia. Spent the night at an 'undisclosed location'. I guess that means the vultures lost track of him at some point. Looks like he's almost here."

Lizbet watched the newscast until Tanji pulled the phone away again. Before she did, Avenall's oh-so-familiar face appeared, then disappeared as an image of the dragons flying overhead filled the small screen. The female newsperson was a little too squee about it for Lizbet to think it was actually news. More likely she was just into the whole idea of dragons and hot-looking elves. Both had become fashionable in the media since Fae Day. Any elf, but particularly one who brought along a herd of dragons, could write his own ticket in Hollywood. She hoped Avenall wasn't one of *those* fae.

No, of course he's not. She rejected the idea completely as she wrinkled her nose in distaste watching Tanji scarf down a spoonful of what looked like baby food. He'd have nothing to do with it. She was assuming that his basic personality had persisted through his reincarnations as Thomas's had. Although she had no proof of it, she believed that Thomas would always do harm because he viewed the world through a single-focus lens like Faolan had done. She also believed that Avenall would always do good because he was as just and thoughtful as Arthur.

Tanji held a spoonful of mashed ick out to her. "You want some of this? Builds up your healing essence."

Lizbet's lips curled in disgust. "Uh, no. It smells like dirty toenails. There's no way I want to be greeting Avenall with that on my breath. It looks like he's going to be here in like five hours, so I'll need to go meet him then. Are you sure your dad's still okay with sticking the dragons out in the barn at your grandfather's old place?"

"Sure. As long as you're still giving the royal guarantee the dragons won't eat the gnomes."

"I am. Avenall said the only reason dragons ever ate gnomes was because the elves made them do it. Apparently, elves don't like gnomes in their gardens any more than anyone else does. It was also good practice for other two-legged creatures they might decide to battle."

"Then you're good to go. Dad cleaned it up a little and made some room. Gramps kept all his junky old 'classic cars' in there, so it's probably big enough for a bunch of dragons and one fine-looking elf."

Lizbet backhanded her friend gently on the shoulder. "Really? Don't you ever give it a rest?"

"Why? You have a problem with this guy? You can tell me to find someone who's more like me all you want, but if I have to wait around for a mixed race, mixed species guy whose parents are going through a divorce, I'm not going to be doing a lot of dating."

Lizbet shook her head. She was more than happy to give Tanji's new crush her BFF stamp of approval as long as it helped her get over the last one. "You know what? I really don't have a problem. Go for it. Just try not to overwhelm him, right? He doesn't just come from a different place. He comes from, like, a whole different time that modern countries mostly left behind centuries ago."

Lizbet and Tanji met up at the bottom of the stairs, hugging the wall to avoid the steady stream of students happy to be heading away from school. "Can you meet us at the barn? I'll give you a call and let you know when we're going to get there."

"Sure. Or I'll just watch it on the news."

"Yeah, there's that. Let's hope they don't figure out where he's landing, or it will be a whole other circus."

There were a lot of kids still hanging around in the parking lot, so Lizbet walked around the side of the school to be out of sight for her disappearing act and to pop her wings out in advance so she'd fly instead of fall when she got there. Even though she'd done it dozens and dozens of times, she was still the tiniest bit afraid she'd disappear into the aether and never be heard from again. But everything went fine. She thought of going to where she'd seen Avenall and poof! Just like that, she was there.

The dragons startled when she suddenly appeared off to the side of their flight path with her scarf and wings flapping. They veered sharply at the same time, synchronized in their movements. Avenall rocked in his seat and grabbed onto the saddle just in time to prevent being spilled off the side.

In the moment before the dragons veered away, she saw him as Morgan had seen Arthur many times: pensive, regal, and intelligent. Despite his young age, he had a look of world-weariness. She had no doubt now that this Avenall was her Arthur. She would trust him with her life. There was no doubt at all.

When the dragons calmed, Lizbet flew closer to Avenall and pulled the scarf away from her mouth so that she could talk to him more easily. Even then, she and the dragons were moving swiftly, and she was unsure her words would reach him before they blew away. "I was going to fly along with you, but it's too cold for me. How can you stand it?" She mimed hugging herself for warmth and shivered as she flew.

Avenall nodded his head. He understood about the cold. Beneath his furs, his hands were icy and his ears felt like they would never be warm again.

She continued. "I'm going to aether myself a little ahead for each step along the way. Just head for me. I'll be a marker for the way to go." She demonstrated what she meant by disappearing and then reappearing several hundred feet in front of the dragon's flight path. She beckoned to them. Although the dragons startled again, Avenall was prepared this time and quickly soothed them as he sent the message to find the girl as she disappeared and reappeared. Soon, they understood and followed this strange beacon as it flashed off and on, leading them onward.

* ~ * ~ *

Lizbet put herself back on the ground for a couple of minutes to give a quick call to Tanji. She had no interest in dropping her phone from flying height. "Yeah, Tanj, about half an hour. See you there." Then she projected herself into the sky again.

What a life, she thought. *I'm using something I don't understand to travel through the air so that I can guide a gaggle of dragons to a cabin where my best friend's father relocates the gnomes and pixies he gathers. And for what? To try to find a person who turned into a tree and heal her before she dies from an arrow wound. Really? And I used to think physics class was a challenge.*

Soon, she was just above the barn. She floated down toward it slowly, hoping Avenall would catch the hint that this was the place to land. He did.

As she headed for the ground followed by the dragons, she saw Tanji pull her car up in front of the barn and get out, then stand there, looking up and saying what looked like "Wow" over and over again, with a probable "Yike!" thrown in for good measure. Mr. Ross exited from the passenger side, and his actions matched his daughter's except with more wows. Lizbet was glad somebody was getting a kick out of this. Because she was exhausted and freezing and could hardly wait to get back home and take a hot shower so she could feel her toes again.

She touched down gracefully, something she had had to practice because it didn't do for a queen to always be falling in the mud when landing, and walked over to greet Mr.

Ross. "You're here to make sure the dragons really won't go for the gnomes, aren't you?"

"Well, I did promise them they'd be safe here. And the last thing this city needs is the gnomes returning to its gardens. There'd be a riot. Plus, the gnomes have insisted on sending a few delegates to check it out for themselves. I'm supposed to go get them when the dragons arrive."

"Go get them then, because I want to get these guys hidden before the local news crews figure out where they landed."

Ron took off in the direction of the small, ramshackle cabin where a gigantic statue of a gnome looked out across a large mess of a garden. The gnome city filled several acres now. Ron had had to purchase additional land throughout Ohio for similar areas as the business grew.

When he'd first prepared the garden, he'd supplied small huts for the gnomes, but they preferred to live underground and there was no changing them. They did use some of the buildings for meeting spots, but they tended to meet on the roof rather than inside. He'd quickly learned gnomes could generally be counted on to do exactly what you didn't want them to do.

He returned with three elder gnomes in tow just as the dragons touched down and folded their broad wings. It was a threatening sight, even though all of them but the black one were no larger than a horse and the smallest was pony-sized. Still, to a gnome, they would be gigantic. The gnomes stood stiff and silent, a surprisingly ungnomelike behavior.

Lizbet walked to Avenall and quietly explained why the gnomes were there. Avenall then turned and walked to each of his dragons in turn, laying his head against the side of theirs affectionately, murmuring to them as he did.

After he'd approached each of the dragons in this way, he turned and said in gnomish, "Please, brave gnomes, come forward. You have nothing to fear from these dragons."

Tanji asked, "Me, too?"

"Not the time, Tanj." Lizbet threw a cautioning glance in her direction.

"Yes, your queen-ness. You sure know how to rain all the heck over a girl's parade when you're being royal."

Lizbet rolled her eyes. Tanji smiled and rolled hers back. Then, Lizbet returned her attention to the gnomes. She'd believed Avenall when he told her that dragons would not harm anything that flew or that walked on two legs unless they were threatened or were being guided to attack, but she couldn't help worrying. There were times she'd wanted to smoke a gnome or two herself just on principal. She wasn't as bothered by them as Eamon, but she definitely got why he disliked them so much. They were like bargain basement knock-offs of The Three Stooges except with bonus bodily noises.

Everyone, including Avenall, seemed to be holding his or her breath as the gnomes moved closer to the dragons. When the largest dragon, the one called Fein, lowered its head to sniff the gnome that stood in front of it, it was all she could do not to run forward, grab the little guy, and run away. But she held back. She had earlier realized she trusted Avenall with her own life. She would have to trust him with the lives of others as well.

When Fein merely continued sniffing, then shoved the gnome in a playful way with his snout, the gnomes loosened up and came forward in a clump. Before anyone had time to react, they'd clambered onto the back of the big dragon and were rooting through Avenall's saddle bags, laughing and having a great time.

Ron gave a wry smile. "Did not see that coming. But that's my usual reaction to gnomes."

"And probably also not the best decision I've ever seen them make," said Lizbet, as she noted the concern on Avenall's face.

"No problem. They've seen what they came to see. And now they can go home." Ron pulled a baggie full of sugar out of his pocket and sprinkled some on the ground. At first, only one gnome raised his head, nostrils twitching. Then the other two caught the scent and followed suit. They forgot about the contents of the saddle bags and slid off the dragon's back in a rush. They chased after the trail of sugar Ron left as he hustled back toward the gnome garden with the whooping, farting, fighting confusion of gnomes following, each bent on scooping up the sugar before his huddle-mate sgot to it.

"I owe him thanks," said Avenall.

Tanji blurted out, "You can thank me and I'll let him know. He's my male parental unit."

"Avenall, this is my best friend, Tanji."

"I'm pleased to meet you Tanji. Please thank your malprental unit for me," Avenall said, stumbling on the unfamiliar phrase. "You are both very kind."

"Sure. And there's no such thing as malprental, although now that you've said it, I'm thinking there should be. I like a fresh new word to play with, among other things fresh and new..."

To stop Tanji from working herself into full flirt mode complete with eyelash batting, Lizbet interrupted. "Yep. Tanji likes words. Especially ones nobody else ever uses or understands. Avenall, we need to get the dragons out of sight. Tanji can confuse you some other time."

"Yes. We must. As you say."

Tanji went to find her father as Lizbet opened the barn door. Avenall walked behind the dragons, silently herding them toward their new home.

CHAPTER TWENTY-ONE

So Glad I Found You

THERE'S NOTHING LIKE A worksheet full of calculus problems to bring a girl back to reality. Lizbet chewed on the end of her pencil, then wrote her answer to the final question and set her pencil down to wait for the rest of the class to finish.

It was difficult to keep her unoccupied mind from the map she carried in her backpack. She reached under her desk, trying to get to it without drawing the teacher's attention. She slowly unzipped the front pocket and eased the map out, then brought it up to the surface of the desk where she flattened it and began to study it intently for the hundredth time over the past week. She turned it one way and then the other, trying to puzzle out Mona's location from the lines here and the squiggles there, but none of it said to her, "Here I am, come get me." By the time she saw the teacher heading for her, it was too late to hide it.

"Moore, what are you up to now?"

"Nothing, sir. I finished my worksheet and got bored, that's all. See?" She pushed the completed worksheet toward him. He reached for the cloth map instead.

"Give me the whatever-it-is. You know the rules. The only thing you do during the last ten minutes of class is get started on your homework. If you finish it, you just sit tight."

"Yes, sir. Sorry." Lizbet watched him move away with the precious cloth square, briefly looking curiously at it, then folding it and placing it on an empty space on his desk as he sat down to keep a watchful eye over the class again.

When the bell rang and she went to fetch the map, he handed it to her, asking, "What in the world can be so fascinating about a badly drawn picture of a pair of shoes in the woods?"

Lizbet couldn't help it. She reached out impulsively and hugged him. It made so much sense, and yet she hadn't seen it in the twist of lines the dryad had drawn. "Thank you, thank you, thank you!"

Lizbet zipped down the stairs and grabbed Tanji by the hand as she hit the landing next to her, tugging hard to make her friend speed up. "We gotta go. I know where Mona is. The answer was just stupid easy, which is why I couldn't get it, obviously."

The girls ran to the car. When they got there, Lizbet stopped to text James before she turned to Tanji and said, "Can you pick James up from in back of your shop? Your dad is dropping him off at the storage room there in about ten minutes. Then, meet me where we found Mona's shoes. I'm too hyped to sit still in the car. I'm gonna fly."

Lizbet closed her eyes, and the wings she'd inherited with her magic burst from her shoulder blades. Just as quickly, she looked toward the sky and followed her gaze upwards, moving toward the stand of woods on the south side of town.

Tanji watched her go, then maneuvered her car out of the school parking lot.

~~*

Above the trees, a black, glinting shape swooped back and forth. As Lizbet got closer, she saw that it was Avenall, again riding the largest dragon. She flew to them and called, "I know where she is!"

"Euphemia? I've been reaching..." Avenall stopped, realizing he could not tell her about his newly discovered powers, powers that needed to stay hidden. "I've been trying to see through the eyes of the forest creatures, but I've seen nothing to help me locate her."

"I know where she is now, so you can follow me in." Lizbet hung there for a moment, getting her bearings as she tried to interpret what she saw below her. When she figured it out, she zipped off toward a small clearing visible about a fourth of a mile into the small stand of woods.

~~*

"Hey guys, I got her," Lizbet called when she heard James and Tanji coming down the trail, breathing hard and moving fast. They entered the small clearing moments later and walked to where she stood near a tree that looked to them like every other tree. She leaned her head against the smooth bark and patted it soothingly like she would pat an upset friend's back during a hug.

James almost did a double-take when he saw Avenall standing next to her. Lizbet was right—there was no way this wasn't Arthur all fleshy again. It was like seeing someone come back from the dead. With an effort, he pulled his attention back to the reason he'd dropped everything and come running. "So, this is Mona?" he asked.

"Yep, it's her, I know it." Lizbet stopped cradling the tree and pointed to a scar in the bark. "Do you see this? It's perfectly round, and there's a different type of wood in there, filling the hole in. That sure looks like the shaft of an arrow to me. How about you?"

James leaned in closer for a better look. "Yeah, it does."

He turned toward the Arthur-elf again, feeling a little spooky déjà vu, when Avenall added, "And it has the bark of the willow, but the leaves of the oak. This tree could not exist in nature. It could only be a dryad."

"Okay, so we've found her—what do we do now?" Tanji blurted out. "I wouldn't have the first idea how to go about healing a tree, and I'm the best healer of all of us. Or if she changed back, I don't think I could help her fast enough to keep her from bleeding to death. Not if that arrow is through her heart like Avenall said it is. What good is knowing where she is if we can't help her?"

Lizbet warned her with her eyes. "Tanj, go somewhere else if you're gonna freak out. Really. I mean it. You're not helping right now, and I bet Mona can hear you."

"You're right. Sorry. I need to get myself together. I'm going back to the car." Before she did, she walked over to the tree and wrapped her arms around the trunk for a moment. "I'm sorry, Mona. But I promise, we're so going to find a way to get you out of this."

Lizbet took James out of hearing range to talk. She hoped Mona wasn't listening in through the plant life in the surrounding woods. Neither she nor James sounded very optimistic. But that didn't mean they weren't going to figure it out one way or the other.

Lizbet made a quick call which involved a lot of head-nodding and soothing words. When she was done, she filled him in.

"Mom wants to come out and be with Mona since we're going to need time to figure this out. We have to be able to spread all our books around us, so pow-wowing in the woods isn't the best idea. You can go back with Tanji to get started, and I'll wait for my mom to get here."

James shook his head. "No way are you staying out here alone with someone running around shooting arrows at people."

Lizbet made a gesture toward Avenall, where he leaned against Fein's side. "You see the broad-shouldered elf and the threateningly large dragon, right? I'm not alone."

James wasn't sure he trusted Arthur's shade the way Lizbet did, but the guy had traveled all the way across the ocean to save Mona. James decided he should stop being overprotective. "Yeah, yeah, you made your point. Avenall, you sticking around?"

"I'll stay as long as my queen has need of me. I have no knowledge to add to your search for healing."

"Yeah, okay. But Lizzie, meet us back there as soon as you can, right?"

"You bet. I'm just glad Mona's not going to be alone out here this evening."

James hurried back down the trail, tossing ideas around with Myrddin's memories as he walked.

~~*

Sheila arrived burdened down by a heavy camping backpack. She greeted her daughter and smiled cautiously at the elf and dragon who stood at the edge of the clearing, then asked her daughter for help.

The two of them set up the backpacking tent she'd strapped onto the pack and stowed her winter sleeping bag inside it. She'd also brought a small camp stove, a lantern, some snacks, a stack of books, and her laptop.

The mouth of the tent faced Mona's tree. They'd set it up only a few feet away. "Okay, that's a lot of stuff. So, you're planning on staying longer than a few hours?" Lizbet said when they had her mom's tent stabilized.

Sheila pulled a bottle of clear liquid from her pack, removed the bubble wrap she'd wrapped it in to cushion it, and held it up for her daughter to see. "Don't worry about me. You remember this, don't you?"

"Yep. Protection spell from James when he thought the gnomes might go after Bobby again. You put it on the doors and windows at night."

"Yes, that's what it is. But I didn't use much of it because the gnomes didn't get up to anything after they helped when the fae Morgan possessed you. So, I'm going to use it to keep Mona and I safe tonight. That way, you can go home and not worry about us. I couldn't get in touch with your father, so you and Bobby are staying at the Ross's."

"Mom, you know whoever shot Mona could still be out here. Plus, there's no guarantee that potion will still be good." She realized she was acting like James had with her. That kind of thing probably wasn't going to fly with her mother, either.

"That's easy enough to test." Sheila flicked her hand to indicate her daughter should back up, then she walked slowly around the tree and her tent, pouring a small stream of the potion onto the cold ground to make a circle. It glowed a cool blue among the leaves. When she was done, she read a few words from the side of the bottle and the glow disappeared. After it did, she said, "Go ahead, see if you can get in without being invited."

Lizbet tried to walk over the line of blue, but her foot stopped where the circle began. Then she tried to hit through it with a broken branch. Once again, the circle stopped it.

"Okay, so physical stuff can't get through," she said. "I'm going for the big guns now. I'm going to try something James taught me. Go stand by Mona. I want to see if this blows the tent over."

Lizbet stood back a few feet and rubbed her hands together for a moment, then separated them quickly, pushing her palms toward the barrier in one smooth movement. Within seconds, she lost her balance backwards, catching herself and dropping to a sitting position with a look of surprise. "Whoa! It blew my own spell back at me."

"Satisfied now, my careful daughter?"

"Yep. I'm good. Particularly since I'm leaving you with a dragon." Lizbet stood up, brushing leaves off the back of her jeans. She waved as she turned to leave. "Night, mom. Night, Mona. Night Avenall."

Sheila turned, and Avenall bowed his head to her in respect, then hunkered down next to the dragon with earphones in his ears, nodding his head to the beat of his music.

CHAPTER TWENTY-TWO
Figure It Out

LIZBET OPENED HER EYES and looked at the clock. It was only 4:30, but she'd woken up every hour or so since going to bed, her mind busy with the problem of Mona. They hadn't made any progress earlier that night. She couldn't sleep, and she was tired of trying.

She sat up and slipped her legs over the side of the bed, feeling around for her slippers. She didn't want to wake Bobby as he slept soundly on a cot beside her in the Ross's guest room. The kid was seriously cute when he was sleeping. All those red curls framing his face made him look like an angel. Not that she would ever admit that to anyone.

She silently traveled down the hall to Tanji's room, hoping to sneak her book of spells away for study, but neither Tanji nor the book were there.

She went downstairs and found Tanji sitting at the kitchen table. The ancient spell book was open before her, and Tanji ran her finger down one of the pages, mouthing the words of the dead language as she read.

"I'd stop speaking what you're reading if I were you. You might accidentally perform the spell. Your dad probably doesn't want any more storms inside the house."

Tanji looked up, surprised. "Shhh. Keep it down, wouldja? There's a great sorceress at work here."

Lizbet slipped into the chair next to her and moved it in close so that she could read over her shoulder. "Spells for immobilizing people? That's a good idea. I mean, if it could freeze her up so that she wouldn't bleed, then there would be plenty of time to heal her, right?"

"Yeah, it makes sense, but it would only paralyze her and keep the essential processes working, so her heart would still beat and the blood would still flow. Which means no solution yet. I've been at it for hours, not including the ones before bedtime, and I'm beginning to feel defeated."

"Yeah, well, join the club. It was a complete accident how I even found out where Mona is. If Mr. Winslow hadn't caught me staring at the map trying to figure it out, she'd still be out there alone. I'm scared we won't have enough time. How long is a freaking fortnight, anyway?"

Tanji picked up her phone and typed the question into search. "Fourteen days, according to the masterminds of the interwebs. How long does that leave us to come up with a solution?"

Lizbet concentrated for a moment. "We were on the cruise ship on Saturday, and it's going on Saturday again now, so...seven days left, tops?"

"That's plenty of time, right? With you, me, and James working on this, we have to be able to solve it. Plus, we can ask Thomas, too. You know how kind of amazing he is with magic. No matter how much you don't like him, we need to ask him."

"I don't want to admit it, but you're right. Will you ask?"

"Sure. I've got the shop this morning and Thomas is working, too. And this book is going everywhere with me until we figure this out. Since I'm crashing at your place tonight, maybe we can all get together and work on it."

"You're staying over?"

"Dad's going to be in the woods to keep Mona company. Didn't James tell you that he was going to hang with dad for some of the night, too? That way Avenall can get some sleep before he takes the second watch."

"No, he didn't mention it."

"No? Well, apparently some bossy fae queen's mom called and said that poor Avenall is stuck playing bodyguard for anybody who stays with Mona out in the woods."

"Oh yeah, that fae queen. Wow, she's a real wench, huh?"

Tanji opened her eyes wide while she performed an exaggerated nod, "Oh yes, that queen is a real wench!"

They tried hard to giggle softly so they didn't wake anyone else up.

When Tanji arrived at the Moore's later that afternoon, Thomas and James trailed behind her. James carried the stack of wirebound notebooks where he wrote Myrddin's spell knowledge as it surfaced. They all took seats around the table, and Tanji ran down the list of ideas she'd had about how to help Mona.

"Here's the way I see it. One—Mona has to get fleshy within the next ten days or she's tree-woman forever. Two—if she gets fleshy, she also gets bloody. Real bloody.

Three—there is no three, because she's already bled to death before we get to three." She tipped her open book of magic toward her slightly as if she was going to read from it, then let it fall back to the table. "After a day of study on the topic while Thomas did most of the work at the shop, that's what I got. One of you two better be a whole lot smarter than I am."

"I got nothin'", James said. "You're right about what happens. The problem is where the arrow hit. We can't heal her fast enough to prevent her from bleeding out. This needs one of Thomas's magical macgyvers. There's no one spell that's going to take care of it." James looked to Thomas. "All we can do is hope that creative brain of yours jumps through some hoops pretty quick and saves the day."

Thomas avoided James's gaze, pretending to be absorbed in reading over Tanji's shoulder. "I need time with the book and the notebooks you created from Myrddin's knowledge. Understand that I can't promise anything."

"Sure, but don't sell yourself short. You've got the best magical mind of all of us," James replied.

Thomas took Tanji's book and began to page through it, stopping here and there. At one point, he asked James to pass him the notebook he was reading. He compared the pages, then moved on. They were all intent on their work. The time passed quickly.

It was getting dark when James stood up and asked, "You want to go for a walk, Lizzie? Get a little chilly air to clear our heads?"

Tanji quickly put in, "I'll go too, since Thomas is still working and might appreciate the time alone."

Thomas stopped her. "No, I'd like you to stay. Knowing you're here helps me focus."

Tanji reluctantly agreed, and Lizbet trailed behind James,

holding his hand until they stopped at the door to get dressed for the brisk air outside.

Thomas took Tanji's hand in his as she sat down, but she pulled it away. "Stop it. I told you I don't want to be with you that way anymore."

"I know. But my surprise is almost ready, and you'll forgive me then for being distracted. I know you will."

"Look, the only surprise I want is that you know how to fix Mona. Right? Keep your mind on that instead of on me. You already missed out on that chance."

Thomas couldn't reveal his secret yet, but he desperately wanted Tanji to reconsider. What he planned he'd done for her as well as for himself. But if he used what he knew to bring Mona back to her flesh state, she might reveal Freoric as the cause of her trouble. Freoric shouldn't have done what he'd done to her, but there can be casualties when working for the greater good. Still, helping Mona might be the fastest route back to Tanji's affections.

"How much longer do we have before nature takes her?"

"Around nine days as of this morning, assuming I got an accurate estimate. I'd say we don't want to push it, so we really need to be rushing in there with the cavalry by Thursday, don't you think?"

Thomas already knew he could cure Mona. It would be simple enough even though it would probably take most of a day and at least one lesser healer to assist. He was stronger in his magic now than any of them knew. Stronger even than James. But he didn't want to help her too soon: he still needed Freoric's service. He couldn't allow Mona to reveal the name of her attacker and have the others wonder about him because he had openly sought the elf's acquaintance. On the other hand, he didn't want to let the half-dryad die and had never intended that she would. He'd only wanted to stop her from communicating.

He could put off healing her for a few more days and still look good in Tanji's eyes. The globe would be filled soon, anyway. After that, he, Freoric, and Tanji would be on their way to the elven compound, and Freoric would have nothing more to fear.

"I'll keep working on this until I have a solution. Can I have the time off work if I need it?"

"Yeah, take whatever time you need. I'll close the shop if that's what it takes. Who cares about the stupid shop until Mona's okay?"

Thomas patted her hand again, and he noticed that she didn't pull it away this time.

CHAPTER TWENTY-THREE
The Dragon's Retort

BEFORE DAWN, THE DRAGONS flew again toward the great lake that lay to the north. They had to be fed at least every other day, and there was no likely food source near except a small herd of dairy cattle. Avenall's new friend, the pretty half-fae Tanji, had told him the cattle were off limits. He wasn't sure what it meant when she said, "Eamon will be wearing you for a hat if you even think about letting the dragons near that herd," but he was convinced he didn't want to find out. Although there was a small lake near the cabin, it was frozen over. While the dragons could certainly thaw it, there were men fishing through holes in the ice who would be endangered if the ice was weakened.

He took the dragons as high as they would fly to make them less visible from the ground. He rode in Fein's mind all the way there so that he could see farther than with his own limited vision. To the east, machines took to the sky and traveled in many directions. He kept the dragons well west of their origin so that they did not spook from sharing the sky with the noisy sky-boats of silver.

When the large lake appeared below, he found a rocky beach on a small island where the dragons were able to fish, feed, and have their freedom. Avenall let them enjoy themselves until the early afternoon when a boat drew nearby and its occupants began taking pictures. He summoned Fein, mounted, and the dragons started their journey back to the barn where they would need to hide once again.

On the way back, he watched the ground with Fein's eyes. As they flew over the area of forest by the queen's village, he looked sharp for any traces of an elven encampment on the ground, but he saw none.

Then, as he urged Fein to the right, toward the barn where they would again hide for the night, Fein abruptly veered left and forced a picture into Avenall's brain. Far below, three humans surrounded a fourth as she tried to enter her car. The fourth was Tanji. He sent a thought picture to the other dragons to circle in wait but gave Fein his head to rush toward the endangered girl.

Tanji startled when an arm came around her neck from behind and a voice told her not to scream. She didn't scream, but she did swing her elbows backwards with as much force as she could muster and pushed off from the side of the car with one leg, hoping to knock her attacker off balance so she could take off running. In the back of her mind, she remembered Eamon telling her that making flowers grow would never afford her much protection. She wished too late she'd delved further into spells that weren't so focused on healing and other practical uses like rainmaking.

It didn't matter much anyway. Her attacker pulled her around, and she faced two others. Kids she recognized as seniors, a year ahead of her. She also recognized the wildness in their eyes: it warned her of the suped up strength, alertness, and sense of invincibility of the chronic duster.

She was in a world of trouble, that was for sure. The guy who had her in a headlock would be dusted up, and there was no way she'd be able to fight him off when he was under the influence.

His voice was loud in her ear. "Where's your dust? You're friends with that uppity queen. She's always got it, so you gotta have it, too."

"Look, I don't use pixie dust for spells. There's too big a chance there'll be side effects. And I can't travel the aether, so I don't need it for that, either. Seriously, I don't have anything you'd want."

"Somebody get her keys and check the car."

The blonde girl, who stood closest to her, pulled her purse away even though Tanji pulled back in an effort to stop her. Her heavy winter coat prevented the strap from scraping her, but it hurt where it had bit into her arm as she resisted.

The girl dumped the contents of the purse on the ground. She picked the ring of keys up from the pile. It took her a long time to find the right key and get it into the lock. Once she did, she started throwing things out of the car and onto the ground, The GPS, the trash bag full of fry wrappers and milkshake cups, the emergency flares and blanket.

"S'nothin here, Greg. She has to have it on her."

The other boy broke out in a scary grin. "I'll frisk her, if you keep her still." The boy started forward, then his eyes widened in fright as they darted to look behind her. He abruptly turned and ran.

"Greg, geez," the girl who was stepping back out of the car said before she also saw something just over Tanji's shoulder and headed away at top speed.

She could feel the kid who had her in a headlock turn, too, placing painful pressure on the arm he'd pinned behind her back. There was a whooshing sound, and he suddenly let go to take off in the same direction as his friends.

She rubbed her injured arm as she turned around, blue sparks traveling along the sore places to help with the pain.

Behind her stood the black dragon, rearing to his full height and breathing a short gout of flame.

When a handsome face wearing a broad smile peeked out from around the dragon's long neck, Tanji forgot her pain and beamed.

～～*

Tanji looked around in both directions before she entered the code for the alarm at the front door of the Magic On Main shop. She'd talked for a while with the new elf in town after he turned up to be her white knight, but she was still feeling a little rattled and didn't want anyone to be able to get into the shop who shouldn't be there.

She'd felt so positive about magic when it returned to the world, sharing Thomas's total enthusiasm. That was part of his attraction. But magic, as Eamon had drilled into them all over the past few months, often has unanticipated consequences. The kids who got hooked on dust were just one way that played out. Her father made his living coming up with solutions for some of the others through

"Ron Ross's Magical Pest Control" service. Even though she enjoyed her own new powers and running what was probably the first real magic shop in the country, she was beginning to understand why some people might have a problem with this new world.

Tanji was surprised to find Thomas already behind the counter, busying himself filling herb packets. He usually didn't arrive until the minute his shift started. Well, at least he'd put the alarm back on so she didn't freak out about it. She was worried he was there early to spend time with her, and she didn't want to get into a fight with him again and put him off on helping Mona. She had to be nice, but not too nice. Not an easy thing to do when you're thinking about a dishy elf instead. Of course, she'd thought Thomas was dishy, too, not so long ago. She pulled herself back into her retail reality and started her shop opening routine. Go along to get along, like her dad often said. She could deal.

"Have you labeled the new stock?"

"No. Just got here. How was school?"

"Same old, same old. I did have myself a little brouhaha with some dusters in the parking lot, but no harm done." She intentionally didn't mention Avenall's part in her rescue.

"Are you hurt?"

"Nah. They were just looking for dust. They figured I'd have some 'cause I'm Lizbet's friend, I guess. I'm thinking about making a sign for the shop, just to be safe, that says we don't have dust on the premises. Some of those kids are really starting to go over the line on what they'll do to get it."

"Too right, they are. Do we have anything on hand we can make a sign from?"

"Yeah, I think so. There's some poster board left over from the signs we made for the grand opening."

"I'm done with the herbs. I'll get on it."

After Thomas placed the new sign in the shop's front window, he went to her and stood a little too near for someone who's just a friend. "I'm so close to being able to reveal everything I've been working on," he said. "I don't know what I'd do if something happened to you. Especially after what happened to Mona, I want to keep you safe."

He looked like he was going to kiss her, but Tanji was saved by the bell as a middle-aged woman entered the shop and started to browse. Tanji extricated herself quickly as she said, "I'll see if she needs anything."

It wasn't comfortable working with Thomas now, not when he acted like nothing had changed. Because it had changed completely, and he needed to understand that— but she worried that if she made a big thing of it, he'd be less focused on helping Mona, and there was no way she was going to be responsible for that.

"Give me a sec, and I'll walk you to your car," Thomas said as he put the broom back on its hanger while Tanji started bundling up to go. "No, I'm good. I can get there under my own steam."

It was clear she was avoiding him. She'd been avoiding him the entire shift, keeping customers or some bit of work she suddenly had to do between them. She'd been angry with him before, but it didn't usually spin itself out this long.

He slipped up behind her quickly and grabbed her by a wrist as she tried to put her mittens on. He stroked the inside of her wrist with his thumb, a faint blue spark traveling along the vein there without her noticing it. "Don't be cross with me, love. My project will be done soon, and I'll be more attentive. I promise."

Tanji looked into his eyes, taking a breath as she readied herself to reply, but her eyes lost focus and she slumped slowly downward before she could respond. Thomas caught her and lay her gently on the ground, then held his hands above her and used his magic to raise her slightly, suspending her inches above the floor as he guided her floating figure into the back storeroom. Once there, he lowered her gently to the ground again and talked to her softly while he prepared the spell.

"I'm sorry for this. But you'd object if you knew, even though it's for your own good. It will help you when we heal your friend, and it will serve you where we're going. Your magic has to exceed the abilities of a half-human sorceress for you be accepted there."

He rolled her over to lie flat on her back, opened her coat, and spritzed the front of her dress with an atomizer he pulled from one of his coat pockets. Then he took a bottle from another pocket and held it up before his eyes. The contents glowed and swirled with the concentrated essence of the wisps. He'd filled the bottle himself that morning from the globe.

He estimated the bottle contained the concentrated magic of two to three of them. They would give her powers beyond those of an elven sorceress when added to her own, but they would not raise her ability above what he had given James. He'd considered giving her more, but he didn't want her to notice an extreme jump in her power and suspect it wasn't natural. Maybe he would reserve a few wisps for his own use to continue to improve her once they were away from here.

He positioned himself at her head, cradling it in his

hands and using a focusing chant to prevent the wisps from being distracted from their goal. He removed the bottle's glass stopper, and the wisps were immediately drawn to the attractant he'd sprayed on Tanji's clothes. They spread out as they lingered over her body, then sunk into it and disappeared, leaving behind only a light blue glow. Within minutes, the glow dissipated. It was done.

Thomas floated Tanji back to the spot in front of the coat hook and tilted her into a vertical position. He placed her feet on the floor and took hold of her wrist again, then sent a pulse to release her from his charm. She immediately snatched her wrist away and said, "Seriously, Thomas? I told you there's nothing between us. Let it go. I don't want us to end up not even being friends."

He let her walk to her car alone as he locked up.

CHAPTER TWENTY-FOUR

Restless

THE POTION WAS BEGINNING to wear off and the gnomes were restless. It wasn't the way of a gnome to be quiet and still for so long. Gurrdenn decided it was time to take action.

Under his instruction, they built their circle of magic around Freoric's encampment as quickly as possible. It had to be a wide circle, because if they got too close to the silo where he camped, the gnomes grew frightened and ran away. Magic, he knew. Gnomes would not be scard of an elf.

So they danced their wide circle. They made the noises and gestures that lay the barrier down. All things could pass through except that which made Freoric. He'd be trapped until the others decided to do something with him. Gnome magic makes strong fences.

When they were done, they stood just outside the circle, making as much noise as possible to wake the assassin so that they could jeer at him when he reached the barrier but could not pass. He was lucky they only planned to laugh at him. They could have treated him as they did game and created a barrier to let the meat pass through but leave the hide behind.

Freoric emerged from his tent with a scowl on his face. His long legs carried him swiftly toward the hooting, farting, burping gnomes. Gurrdenn wanted to see the look on his face when he hit the barrier. He would laugh then.

But it didn't happen. There was no shock, no barrier, no laugh. The elf just kept coming. The magic which had always worked before failed them now.

The gnomes turned and ran; all but Trerrfrn, whose back was turned because he'd dropped his pants and exposed his small bottom to the elf as a sign of his disrespect.

He didn't have time to pull his pants up before the knife came down.

~~*

It had been the same each day since the gnomes started watching Freoric.

Gurrdenn would step out of the woods at the back of the Moore's yard with his fellow spies. They would stand at attention—or as close to attention as a gnome could be said to stand—while Eamon eyed them suspiciously.

"Well, anything to report today?"

"Elf hunt. Elf eat. Elf sleep."

"He met with no one?"

Gurrdenn would shake his head or sometimes say, "Thomas," and them spit in disgust. "Bad friends. Bad Thomas.

Eamon would become frustrated. Everyone knew

Thomas was too friendly the elf because of his fascination with his race. "I don't believe you're keepin' an eye on him! Are ye sure you havnae been sneakin' off to play games while Freoric skulks around town?"

Gurrdenn shook his head. "Elf hunt. Elf eat. Elf sleep."

But today, the gnomes didn't show up. Eamon waited through the appointed time, even gave it an extra hour. Maybe the spell had worn off, and they'd gone chasing rabbits or the glints of sunlight on a creek.

Gnomes! He was disappointed in himself for suggesting them in the first place. He should have known they wouldn't be reliable.

Tanji sat in her car, trying not to be obvious as she waited for Avenall to return with the dragons. Although she'd tried to focus at school, her brain kept betraying her by drifting off to thoughts of the good-looking elf who'd shown her his chivalrous side the day before. He'd promised she could take a ride with him after he brought the dragons back from feeding today. She didn't know if she was more excited about riding a real dragon or about wrapping her arms around the dragon tender's waist while she did.

She got out of the car and leaned far back on the chilly hood, resting on her mittened hands, to watch as Avenall brought the dragons down, snowflakes starting to swirl around them. He took his earphones out of his ears and waved.

After he landed, he called, "Let me settle the young ones in the barn, and then Fein and I will be glad to show you the sky."

He was very careful with her, making sure that she

mounted safely and was firmly seated before he signaled to Fein to climb. Even then, she grabbed him hard around the middle and gasped as the dragon took the air.

She loved it. It was amazing. She forgot about her arms him. In fact, she forgot about the handsome elf completely as the dragon swooped through the gently falling snow and took her on the most amazing roller coaster ride of her life.

She didn't realize she was freezing until Avenall helped her scramble down once they were back on the ground. She laughed against the cold. "Man, I need to get some heat going right now. There are icicles hanging off my ears! Is there any heat in the barn?"

"The dragons warm the barn as needed. I could have them warm it for you."

"Nah, I can warm up in the car. It will probably be better than a draughty old barn, anyway."

"I've never ridden in a car, nor even upon a cart. Is it much different than traveling by horse?"

"Uh...yeah. I'd guess it is. Not as much fun as riding a dragon, though. But if you want, I could give you a ride. You can get going a lot faster than I think your dragons travel, and you don't have to be freezing to do it."

"I would appreciate being warm. Let me place Fein in his stall and make sure the dragons are comfortable. Then, I would be happy to ride within your car."

The car was toasty warm by the time Avenall finished up in the barn. It took him a moment to figure out how the handle worked, but he'd watched her when she'd entered her car the day before, and he quickly discovered the mechanism. As he entered the car stiffly, ducking low to avoid bumping his head, he said, "I only wish I had some way to be sure the dragons won't be disturbed."

"Oh yeah, the local news. They've been sniffing around

the area, haven't they? I could do a charm if you want—I've got one that prevents anyone getting in but not anyone getting out. That way, if they had to escape, they could."

"You are a powerful sorceress."

The edges of her mouth quirked at the compliment. "Powerful enough, I guess. But the charm's not really that tough to do once you know how. Be back in a jiff."

She hopped out of the car and made a circuit around the barn, then drew a mark in the snow to the right of the barn door.

She handed him the stick she'd used to draw the charm. "When you get back, you just have to repeat the mark on the other side of the door with that stick, and the spell will break. Don't forgot that part, though, because otherwise, you won't be getting in there tonight. But if you do lose the stick or something, the spell will wear off sometime tomorrow anyway."

"The mark, what is it?"

"Just a question mark." Avenall's expression told her he was puzzled. "It's like this..." She took her gloves off, wet a fingertip in the melting snow on the back of her glove, and drew a question mark on the window.

"I do not know this mark. What is its meaning? Is it old magic?"

"No, it's not magic at all. It's just punctuation. You use it when you write out a question. Do you know how to write?"

Avenall hung his head. "Yes, in the elven tonue. I was educated by my mother in it when small, before my magic bloomed. But your language? No. Few dragon tenders have any education. Elves do not enter schooling until it is know what our magic will make us. Dragon tenders take our orders, and we talk to the minds of the dragons. Learning would be wasted on us."

"You speak at least three languages, right? And you taught yourself French and English, right? I don't think education would be wasted on you."

"What question did you ask when you made your spell?"

She cocked an eyebrow at that, and she couldn't keep the flirtiness out of her voice. "Oh, I think there's a lot of questions I could ask, don't you?"

"Questions you would ask me?" he said.

"Yes."

"What would you ask?"

She hadn't thought he'd call her bluff. He didn't seem to understand dumb stuff you say when flirting. She drew a blank, then said, "Well, I like your dragon claw. Do dragons shed them? Is that how you got it?"

"No, they do not shed them. The claw I wear came from a great dragon which died many years ago. He was Fein's sire. He was lucky to live in a time when there was no war among the fae."

"Do you have any others? I'd love to have one."

"No. They are rare. I was given one as the mark of the dragon tender, but I traded it for my music player because I already had this one and wished to wear it instead. It belonged to my master, Durian. It is precious to me. Were it not, I would gladly give it to you in gratitude for giving me and the dragons a place to stay."

"You don't owe us anything. Papa Ross is cool that way. You ready for that ride? Because if you are, you need to snap that belt around your waist. Ohio's got seat belt laws. And you may not think so, but I *always* do what people tell me to." She smirked out the window as she told such a bold lie.

Avenall looked at his waist, but he didn't understand.

Tanji leaned toward him, "I'll do it." She pulled the sections of the belt across his lap and showed him how they snapped together. She thought it was sexy at first, but when she breathed in while close to him, she caught on to the reality that he was living in a barn without a shower or a washing machine. Okay, that was going to need a fix real fast. Definitely not sexy.

So, it would be a quick dash around town to show Avenall the sights and, as soon as they got out of the car, an even quicker text to James with an urgent request for help with elf-boy's hygiene. Because he might be hot, but she wasn't giving him a pass on grooming. He was going to get up close and personal with human hygiene standards real fast. For his own good, of course.

James knocked on the barn door, then opened it and peered inside, calling, "Avenall, hey, it's James."

Avenall responded from high in the hayloft at the other side of the barn. "I didn't know you'd be visiting this night."

"Neither did I. Tanji called and insisted. There's something I'm supposed to help you with that only another guy should mention."

"This is...?"

"Apparently it's been a while since you've had a bath or washed your clothes. Girls get nuts about that kind of thing."

"It is true I have not bathed regularly since I became a dragon tender. I was given leave only once a fortnight to bathe and to clean my garments. I had hoped that such an arrangement could be made here at the barn. There is a trough I could use."

"Yeah, well, we've got this fancy thing called a shower in every house these days. And washing machines. And since Tanji told me to make you familiar with both, I'm doing it. That girl can be insistent! It's always better to just go along. So come on down, bring any clothes you have that you're not wearing, and I'm going to treat you to an all-expenses-paid trip to my tiny bathroom followed by this small town's premiere laundromat. I may even have some old clothes that will sort of fit you if you tuck the pants into your boots. Because I'm tall, but I'm not elf tall."

James tried not to gawk as Avenall climbed down from the loft and came toward him. It was spooky to see Arthur's head on Avenall's classically elven body. Arthur had been much shorter and stockier, with Avenall's blond hair and a red-blond, wooly beard that grew high up onto his cheeks. It helped him as a leader that so much of his otherwise naturally pleasant face was hidden. It had allowed him to look more severe when it was called for. Avenall simply looked kind and open. But James didn't allow himself to believe that Avenall was a pushover. A pushover wouldn't have stolen a herd of dragons from an elven compound. And there was that little thing he could do with a mental push, too, that he'd been keeping hidden.

He had to ask him. He had to verify what he'd seen.

As Avenall walked from stall to stall, checking to make sure the dragons would be fine before he left, James blurted it out. "When I saw you on the news while you were still on the ship, I thought I saw you force someone to walk away from the dragons."

"I don't understand. I was in no confrontation when on the ship."

"I didn't mean you got into it with anyone. I mean you used your magic to make him do what you wanted."

Avenall was still facing away, so James couldn't see his face, but he felt sure he saw tension in Avenall's shoulders when he replied, "You have been listening to old women's stories for frightening children. Dragon tenders have no power to enter the minds of people, only the dragons and other animals. Still, it is a sentence of death to even try. I think you must be mistaken."

The black dragon shifted abruptly in its stall and then reared to its hind legs, looking directly at James as a small puff of smoke left its snout. Avenall turned his attention to the dragon, not speaking, but James was sure he was communicating to it. It lay back down after a moment.

It worried him that Lizbet was convinced this guy was her great friend Arthur and that she could trust him with anything. He was sure that Avenall had not only puppet-mastered the man on the boat but had now also lied about it. James wanted to believe that Avenall was his old friend born again, but he had reservations about a less-than-honest guy whose emotions could stir up dragons.

But whatever. Tanj would be way up in his face if the guy didn't get his shower. First things first.

CHAPTER TWENTY-FIVE
I Can Help

IN THE EARLY MORNING of the third day after Thomas told her he'd find a way to save Mona, Tanji opened her front door to an insistent knock. Thomas stood there, blowing into his ungloved hands to warm them.

"I've figured it out," he said. "I just need to slow the metamorphosis from tree to human. That will give you, James, and Lizbet time to heal the human parts as the change happens. It will be difficult, and it will require enormous focus, but if we work together, we can heal Mona. I'm sure of it."

Tanji couldn't stop herself. She lunged toward him, grabbing him around the neck in a gigantic hug. One thing you could say for Thomas: he smelled good. Like soap and spiced tea.

"Thomas! Can we do it today? Can we do it now?"

He placed his hands at her waist, gently returning her

hug. "Yes. But we'll need to stop by the shop and create a potion to douse her as she changes. I'll need lavender, valerian, and shisandra. Fortunately, we stock all of that. And we'll need a large sprayer. The kind they use for pesticides, one with a metal wand. I'll need to be able to reach all of her branches as we work."

Tanji slipped into her coat and grabbed the car keys off the hook behind the door. "Have you told Lizbet?"

"No. I thought I would leave that for you."

"Oh yeah, forgot—Lizbet doesn't consider a call from you a priority. Buddy, if you can get Mona fixed up, things could definitely change with that girl. I know she'll finally forgive you."

He was no longer concerned what the Queen of the Fae thought of him. He had already wasted too much time trying to win her favor. In the days that had gone by while he pretended to study healing to save Mona, he had refined his special spell, the enormous, world-changing spell that would place the fae back in their rightful place and allow him to take Tanji to their new home among the elves. As he worked, he had realized how unlikely it was that the elves would follow a human queen when their power in the world had been restored.

Thomas had prepared Queen Morgan for burial. The true queen was already dead.

~~*

Sheila watched as her daughter, Tanji, and James gathered around the trunk of the tree that was Mona in her nature form. Thomas walked behind them with a plastic backpack sprayer wetting the trunk of the tree, its branches, and the ground where the roots sank into the earth. He slipped the wand into the holster at his side and said, "That's it. We're as ready as we'll ever be."

Lizbet reached to each side to grab and squeeze her friends' hands. "Mona, I know you can hear us, so just do whatever Thomas says. He's going to guide you through this. The rest of us are here to help. And I'm really sorry in advance because I know it's going to hurt..."

She let go of the others' hands and lay her palms on the smooth bark of the Mona-tree, then closed her eyes. She breathed in the soothing lavender scent left by Thomas's potion and concentrated on it in order to focus. The others followed her lead.

Thomas spoke quietly. "Mona, I'll take over the trans-formation after you initiate it. Don't push it. Just start it, and then allow me to take charge. You may fear that you'll be trapped mid-transformation, but I assure you, I won't let that happen." He lifted his hands up and closed his eyes, taking a long breath, then slowly let it out. "Start trans-forming now. Then stop immediately." With those words, a fine blue glow started in his palms and grew to encompass the tree. The branches shivered and then were still.

With his eyes still closed and his body enveloped in the same glow that surrounded the tree, he spoke softly to the group around him. "Tanji, focus on healing the heart as it forms. The transformation will take place from the inside out. James, Very slowly remove what's left of the arrow as Tanji's sorcery heals her from the core. Prevent as much blood flow as you can to give Tanji time to repair the tissues. If you remove the arrow too quickly, there's danger from blood loss. Only a millimeter at a time will do."

Sheila watched and listened as the young people began their task. She wasn't sure what her daughter's role was, other than to be there for her friends. Lizbet was politically powerful among the fae, but her magic was nowhere near as strong as the magic of the others. Sheila understood when Lizbet patted the tree affectionately and lay her cheek against the bark, murmuring words of reassurance. Lizbet was there to calm and to care as much as to be ready to lend her magic. Her daughter was good at that.

Sheila was startled by a scuffling at her side. Looking down, she realized she'd been holding her breath as she watched the process begin. Eamon had slipped in beside her while she stood fixed in place and looked up at her solemnly.

"Aye, it's a dreadful thing, not knowin'."

"Yes, it is. It really is."

They didn't talk any more as they listened to Thomas's infrequent instructions to ease off or move attention here or there. The blue light sometimes swirled, sometimes darkened, sometimes stabilized. Sheila didn't know what any of it meant, but she watched as the tree became more and more shaped like her friend.

The process took several hours. When it was done, Mona lay on the ground unconscious but breathing. Tanji waved one hand over the last mark of the arrow above the half-dryad's left breast. James turned his head away from the naked woman, and moved to Sheila to take the blanket she offered. He carried the blanket to Lizbet. She and Tanji wrapped Mona up in it the best they could and waited for her to wake.

Thomas walked to Sheila. "She'll be fine," he said. Sheila hugged him tightly. She had no words to express her thanks.

When Mona sat up and looked around, she recoiled automatically at the sight of Thomas hugging her friend, then quickly hid her feelings. Lizbet saw her reaction and wondered about it, but she kept her wondering to herself.

~~*

Sheila fluffed the pillows again and fussed with Mona's blankets. "Are you sure everything is okay? That you don't need anything?"

"Sheila, I'm fine. I don't need mothering," her friend replied. "I'm exhausted, and I have some terrible memories, but what you've already done for me—staying with me, reading to me, talking to me and keeping me focused on human things—what you, Ron, and Avenall did, it made all the difference in the world to me. It kept me fighting."

"Well, we missed you." Sheila squeezed her hand and then stood to go. "Sleep tight."

"I will. But first I need to talk to Lizbet privately, as my queen. Could you ask her to come in?"

"Of course. But don't talk too long. You really do need your rest."

Mona rolled her eyes weakly but smiled, too.

Lizbet appeared in the doorway within a few minutes. "Mom says you needed to talk to me, but I'm under strict orders not to upset you or let you get too tired. So, I'm doing that. I may be a queen, but I'm a queen who can still be grounded, right?"

Mona nodded. "It's a short conversation, I think. I know you want to know what happened to me, but I didn't want to talk in front of everyone."

"Was it Freoric who shot you?"

"Yes. I think he wanted to keep you from communicating with the fae in Europe."

"I think so, too, since the elves have pretty much sent everyone into hiding over there now. I'm sorry he hurt you."

"I don't blame you. I blame him. But there's more going on. It's not just what's happening in Europe. There's something happening right here. And Freoric is working with the person who's responsible for that."

"So spill!"

"I don't want it to be true—I thought we were friends, and I know it will hurt Tanji, but Thomas is working for the elves. And he's doing something that will cause a lot of harm."

"It's no big secret I don't trust Thomas, but he's the one who healed you. Why would he do that if he was plotting against everyone?"

"I know he healed me, and I wouldn't have survived otherwise, but Oriane is sure the elves have plans that Thomas is carrying out. They've got her locked up in a cell, and she risked a lot to communicate that information for you. I can't imagine that she's wrong about it. I just don't have details." Mona yawned but fought against it. "You need to be careful about Thomas and probably want to find out where he goes and what he does when he isn't around any of you."

"That won't be easy. He and Tanji broke up, although they seemed pretty friendly again after the healing...so, maybe not. Who knows? I think James and Eamon will already be busy trying to track down Freoric, so...I guess that leaves me to sneak around and try to figure out what my 'grandson' is up to."

"Tell me you're not thinking of doing that on your own."

"No, I can probably find a helper among my loyal subjects who has all of the requisite skills. Thank goodness people keep pledging themselves to me, or I'd end up having to be just another kid running for student council." Lizbet sighed. "Man, if only."

CHAPTER TWENTY-SIX
Sneakin' Around

TANJI GINGERLY RUBBED THE smallest dragon, Mer, behind the ears and he responded with a low growl that sounded more like a purr than a warning.

"He likes you," Avenall said.

"I like him too. He's gorgeous, isn't he?" Tanji replied, kneeling down to get a better look at the dragon's face, "But my question is, is it safe to stand this close? Will he just flame up or something when I'm not looking?"

"Young dragons need to learn to control their fire, but they learn quickly. Their mothers are good teachers. That's why they don't take the young dragons away for training for a year or two. Mer is three years old and recently started training to the saddle. That is why he's so much smaller than the others. He'll end up being the size of a horse in a few years. Fortunately, Mer will never again have to be subject to the dragon riders and their rough ways."

"So, they're some pretty rude 'tude dudes?" Tanji asked. Avenall looked confused.

"Not nice people?" she clarified.

"True. The dragon riders are most certainly rude 'tude dudes." Avenall's mouth shaped itself around the words awkwardly, then he grinned.

Tanji grinned back. So, there's some playfulness under that hotness, too.

She was sure there might have been an eyes-lingerin-gon-each-other moment if her phone hadn't started playing "God Save The Queen". She pulled it out of her purse and reluctantly walked a little way away from the dragons and their dragon tender.

"Hey, Lizness, what's up? How's Mona doing?"

"She's doing okay, but...are you still with Avenall out at the barn?"

"Yeah, I'm getting up close and personal with his charges. They are uber-cool."

"Okay, stay there, please. James and I are on our way to you."

Tanji snuck a glance at Avenall, whose attention was on the dragons now. She smirked. "You so definitely don't have to twist my arm on that one, especially now that elf-boy has discovered shampoo. See you in a bit."

Tanji turned back to all five of the fascinating creatures she'd come to visit.

Lizbet materialized in front of the barn holding tightly to James's hand. It was a beautiful night, cold but with a clear sky full of stars. Although her breath frosted in front of her face, she wished they could stand there and enjoy the backwoods beauty for a while. But no, Avenall had come for a reason, and they needed his help if they were to find and capture Freoric and bring him to justice. She still had no clue what to do about Thomas.

She hadn't even told James about him yet. She couldn't bear to reveal that secret twice to people who cared about him. She would tell James and Tanji together.

When she entered the barn with James holding the door for her, Eamon's familiar voice sounded from behind, saying, "Hold the door, gruagachs comin' through." Eamon and Hamish buzzed by her in a rush only to stop dead and gape at the dragons on the other side of the door once they'd passed her.

"What did I tell ye, Hamish? Dragons, right?" He turned back to Lizbet. "No other place we could meet, then? Not that I've anything against dragons, mind you, but Hamish here..."

Lizbet suppressed a smirk. This was a whole new side to Eamon she'd first seen when they went to meet Avenall. She did her best not to let on she knew whose fear he was really expressing when she asked, "Hamish, are you too afraid of the dragons to stay and talk with us? Because Eamon could let you know later if there's anything we need your help with. I'm sure Eamon isn't afraid of a few dragons."

"I'm right sure if Eamon can bear being close to the dragons, then I can do the same." Hamish glared at his companion, but Eamon looked innocently away.

"Good. Because you're both very important to this discussion. You have a useful way of getting around without being seen."

James used some simple magic to move a few bales of hay into the center of the barn. While he worked, Tanji blew starweed into the air to brighten the dark corners.

"If you wish, my queen, the dragons can provide us with warmth without fire. But they will need to draw close to us."

"Are you sure it's safe?"

"I assure you again, dragons who are not trained to war would never attack a human or a fae. Their natural diet is fish and four-legged prey. They do not attack creatures that fly or walk on two legs. The dragons will protect me and my friends, not harm them. I promise you, it will be safe."

Lizbet looked to the gruagachs, neither of whom seemed reassured. "Is it okay with you guys?"

Eamon replied gruffly, "If Hamish doesn't mind, I don't mind."

Hamish replied equally as gruffly, "If Eamon doesn't mind, I don't mind."

"Okay, that's settled. Everybody take a seat, and Avenall will join us once he's got the heat going."

As Tanji passed Lizbet to find a seat on the bales, she leaned into Lizbet's ear and whispered, "He's already got the heat on." Lizbet didn't want to encourage her too much, but she couldn't help smiling. Leave it to Tanji to remind her that not everything is grim. She just hoped that Tanji would be able to keep her own spirits up once she knew what Mona had revealed about Thomas.

Lizbet looked around the group assembled on the bales and at the glittering dragons in a ring behind them. She shifted her weight way back onto her own bale and crossed her legs, then took her gloves off and set them aside. It was already beginning to feel warmer in the small barn as the dragons breathed heavily behind them.

"Okay, so, all of you are the people in this town I can completely trust. And every one of you has to promise that anything I tell you here tonight goes nowhere."

There was a chorus of sures and ayes.

"Good. Because we have a lot to talk about. First, we were right to think Freoric was the one who shot Mona. She confirmed it."

"I can't say I'm surprised," Eamon responded.

"No, I don't think any of us are, really. So we can go ahead with grabbing him and hanging onto him until I can call a proper court." Lizbet shifted on her bale, fidgeting with a piece of straw she rolled between her fingers. "Next, what Avenall came here to tell us in addition to helping us find Mona," she said, tipping her head slightly toward the elf who stood stiffly behind the circle, "is that the elves are planning to go to war against the humans. Which sounds crazy, except…" Lizbet broke off then and took a deep breath. "…except that they have someone here working with Freoric on something they think will even things out. And it's Thomas. He's on their side. I'm sorry. Mona just told me about it." Her eyes darted first to Tanji and then to James.

Tanji shook her head. "No way! Thomas is a stick in the mud and way too serious, but he's not a spy for the elves."

"Tanj, he is. Like I said, I'm sorry. Elder Shan of the French compound has Oriane caged in his jail. He bragged to her about something big 'the Abomination' was going to be doing for the elves. I have to believe that if an elder told her this when he thought she couldn't communicate it to us, it must be true."

Avenall moved into the circle of bales, drawing everyone's eyes in his direction. He asked, "Shan has captured Oriane?"

"I'm sorry to tell you this way, but yes. He has."

Avenall cast his gaze around the circle slowly, making contact with each of the humans and fae as he spoke. "Elder Shan is my father. I well know how he will behave." He waited for a moment, but no one reacted. They waited for him to continue. "If he has Oriane, who is my friend, and he has told her this, it makes much sense. He's a bitter man. A man disappointed and shamed that his only son was born with the magic of a dragon tender rather than a warrior. What he cannot take out on me now, I have no doubt he would gladly throw in my friend's face if only to taunt her with her inability to act. I'm glad she found a way to help you."

"Thank you," Lizbet said, then added, "Does this change whether or not you can help us? Shan being your father?"

Avenall held his head high. "No. I've had much time to think about my choices since I left the compound. He lost his right as my father years ago through his own actions. He is not my father in anything but name, and I reject him as my elder. I pledge myself to you, and I will do as you command."

"Well then, first—I don't command. Get it? I don't command. It's more like a..." Lizbet's forehead scrunched up in thought. "It's really more like a round table here. I suggest, and then I hope it's a good idea that you want to get involved with. Do you know what I mean?" Her eyes darted quickly to meet James's, and his eyebrows lifted just the slightest as he acknowledged their shared understanding of Avenall's origins.

"A sharing of responsibility? Like the first Elf Councils?"

"Yes. a lot like that." *Or the everlasting symbolic one you created as Arthur*, she thought. "We talk about it, we make a plan, and then we agree on exactly what will happen."

"Then I will gladly be a member of this circle and pledge myself to support all of its members."

"Aye, as do I," Hamish chimed in.

"Good. Because we have a real problem on our hands and it's going to take every single one of us to figure out what to do about it. First up, we need to figure out how to deal with Freoric because he'll be easier to talk about than some of the other stuff. It's not like he's tried to make friends here since he followed James and Thomas from London. And I've never been super-thrilled that the only ambassador to the elves I've got is also an assassin."

Eamon said, "We haven't managed to gain any information on him, but the gnomes found his camp in the woods, and they've kept him in sight. However, they didn't report at the scheduled time today."

"Do you know why?" Lizbet asked.

"I assume they're off behaving like gnomes."

"Yeah, well, can you find out for sure instead of making assumptions? They may have learned something."

"Aye, I'll go lookin' after we're done here."

"Perfect, thanks. And take Hamish with you. I don't want anyone working alone right now. Then, as soon as you know the location of his camp, let James know." She turned to Avenall. "Would you work with James when it's time to go after Freoric?"

"Yes, I'd be happy to work with James. I'm honored to be asked."

"Okay, so, up next...we have to make some decisions about what to do about Thomas."

Tanji crossed her arms as a pained look crossed her face. "I don't like to think that Thomas is involved in anything bad, but he's been telling me for a while that he's working on some secret. He kept saying it would be something I'd really like and well—maybe what he's been talking about is some big, bad, magical thing for the elves. He almost always gets it wrong when he tries to figure out what makes me happy."

"Look, Tanj, I saw how you sorta got close to him again

after Mona. I know it's rotten of me to ask, but can you pretend that you're okay with being back together just until we figure this out? I was going to ask Hamish to spy on him, but then I realized Thomas would feel him lingering around. I don't want to put him in danger."

Hamish began to protest, but Lizbet cut him off. "No, Hamish. I think this is the right choice. So...Tanj?"

"Everybody hear that?" She looked around the circle, ending with Avenall, her gaze lingering on him longer than the others. "I'm going to be *pretending* I'm back with Thomas. Totally faking it." Tanji turned back to Lizbet with a look of concern. "Can I tell my dad that?"

"No. Not this time. It's fae business, and I don't want anyone who isn't fae knowing. They might try to handle it with human methods. That's not a good idea since I don't think the elves have any problem going after humans now. I'm not even telling my mom much except that I'll be investigating what happened to Mona. I think it helps to have a little of the fae tricksiness when you're trying to pretend you don't know what someone's been up to. Mom doesn't have it in her. I don't think your dad does, either."

"Yeah, that's for sure. When he suspects me of something, it's all over his face. Thomas would make him in a minute."

"So, that's it. James, can you keep a locator spell going somewhere so that we can know where Thomas is all the time?"

"Can do. I have some small stuff he left behind when he moved that I can use for the owned object."

"Good. So, looks like we have a plan of attack: Tanji, just keep your eyes and ears open and let me know if you think anything weird is up. Don't do anything about it, okay? Eamon and Hamish, you're going to see if the gnomes still know where Freoric is, and Avenall—if you don't mind making a quick trip back to your hometown tomorrow, we've got a friend to get out of a cell."

Avenall's face lit up. "Thank you. But before we are through here, I must also mention the wisps."

"What about 'em?"

"Have you not noticed? The wisps around us are moving. And from the air, you can see that they are moving in one direction—toward the woods where you found Euphemia."

"Okay, so—what does that mean?"

"I am unable to tell you the meaning. It does seem a strange portent, especially when a wizard has been working in secret in this town."

"I'm not really into portents, to tell you the truth." She looked to her boyfriend. "James, you or Myrddin got anything on this one?"

James looked thoughtful for a moment and then said, "Maybe. You know how Thomas used wisps to give me magic? Maybe he's calling them here to make himself stronger. What he did for Mona was pretty intense. I don't think I could have done it even if he told me how, but he didn't even break a sweat. But even then, he couldn't be taking in that many wisps. I mean, he'd start fracking glowing. The human body can only contain so much magic before it leaks. Other than that—I don't think you could make an army out of wisps. They don't have any physical form to stick them together. But who knows what Thomas could macgyver? We could be looking at a bedknobs and broomsticks situation."

"Yike on either one of those possibilities! Maybe I'm rethinking that thing where I just asked my best friend to pretend to be his girlfriend so she can spy on him."

"No biggie, girl. Thomas would never hurt me no matter

what else he's up to. He may not be the world's most attentive boyfriend, but he worships me. Who wouldn't, right?"

"Okay. But just, you know, be aware of that whole may-
be-an-evil-genius-super-powerful-wizard thing."

"I hear ya. I got this. We done?"

Lizbet nodded. "I think we are." She turned to Avenall
and added, "I'll come pick you up tomorrow. I'm assuming
you know where they'd be keeping Oriane?"

"Yes, there are two cells in the bottom floor of the council
house. She would be in one of them."

"Okay, good. I can't aether in to a place unless I've seen
it or I'm with someone who has. Don't ask me how it works
beyond that, though."

Tanji asked, "You guys need a ride home?"

"I guess we'll get back the way we came. I'm pretty sure
mom thinks we're still in the family room, so if she hasn't
noticed we left, I don't need the sound of the front door
tipping her off."

The girls hugged goodnight. "Maybe I'll help dragon-boy
here get the little dragons tucked up for the night and then
head home myself."

Lizbet took a pinch of pixie dust from a pouch she wore
around her neck with Morgan's medallion and blew it off
her fingers toward James before she took his hand and they
disappeared. The gruagachs took their leave immediately
after and sped off into the night to get to work finding the
missing gnomes.

Their departure left Tanji to fall into step beside Avenall
as he followed the dragons back to their stalls. She knew
that he was communicating what he wanted with his magic.
That idea was both fascinating and scary. That was some
kind of power, if it let you control a bunch of dragons.

"So, your friend Oriane—how close are you two, anyway?"

Avenall looked sad for a moment, and then, without looking at her, said, "We are very close. It is my understanding she feels about me as a mother would."

"I see. You did hear that part about where I'll just be *pretending* to be Thomas's girlfriend, right?"

Avenall turned to look at her then. She gave him her most impish smile. He looked shy for a moment, maybe even a little embarrassed, and then he smiled an impish smile back.

～～*

"This way, Hamish. It looks like the wee cretins went through here." Eamon followed the low trail of bent grasses and broken flowers to walk through a bog ripe with the smell of rotting vegetation. "I have to say this for them, it will keep the elf from picking up their scent, that's for sure. Assuming he doesn't question why a bog's gotten up and started walkin' about."

Eamon pulled up short on the far side of the bog and Hamish nearly bumped into him as he did. In front of them, three gnomes sat rocking back and forth in the dirt, heads in their hands and hands covering their faces, around a mound of freshly dug earth.

"Gurrdenn, what's gone on here? You were supposed to report back."

Gurrdenn replied in gnomish. "Trerrfrn dead. Many pieces." The gnome lowered his head and shook it slowly back and forth. "So many."

Recognizing the reason for the disturbed earth, Eamon

asked the next logical question, although he felt sure he already knew the answer. "Who killed him?"

"Elf."

"Why didn't you come back right away and let us know? We would have been right out after him."

Gurrdenn's eyes flashed anger. "Many pieces."

Hamish prodded Eamon and whispered, "I think they had to find all the parts before they buried him? You know how the gnomes are about getting their dead buried and back home in the earth quickly."

"Och, sorry, I..."

Gurrdenn sat back down and joined the ring of mourners, motioning to Eamon and Hamish to join them.

The gruagachs sat with the gnomes in silence, waiting for daylight when the mourning period would end and they could follow the gnomes to Freoric's camp.

CHAPTER TWENTY-SEVEN

Hole in the Earth

T HE INSIGNIA ON THE wooden box on Shan's desk glowed, signaling that a message from the assassin had arrived. He slid the top of the box aside and removed the small, folded manuscript within. As he read, he smiled. The event he'd been waiting for would happen this very night.

But he was displeased when Freoric described the arrival of the dragons. He forced himself not to dwell on it and turned his mind back to the completion of all he had planned through the work of the Abomination. When it was done, the fae would have no choice but to turn away from their human queen and back to the old ways. The elves would once again have the rule of the forests and a respected voice in fae leadership.

Still, he relished the thought of making the boy pay for his betrayal. His mother would have sheltered him just as she sheltered him from Shan's wrath when the shame of his magic became known, but Shan knew better what to do with such a child. All residents of the compound would watch as Shan swung the blade, reminding all the sons of the elves of the power of the ancient ways.

It cheered him to picture his son's undoing. He had to share it with someone, someone who would care and cry now that the boy's mother no longer could. He stood and strode confidently out the door and down the stairs to the prison below him.

Oriane lay in a corner of her cage. Her energy, the very force of her life, was fading from being so little connected to the soil. If she didn't unite with the earth again soon she'd become so weak she wouldn't be able to initiate a return to her nature form. Soon after she could no longer transform, she would die. When the door to her cell opened, she didn't even try to pull herself up to see who had entered.

It didn't matter. She knew his voice.

"Are you weakened, dryad? I'd hoped you would live long enough to see my son returned to the compound to have justice served upon him. It will be a shame if you are not there at the end. Perhaps I will have the guards bring a pot of earth for you to revel in and regain your strength. But only if you please me."

She gathered what strength she had to pull herself up and sat facing him, her back against the bars of her cage. "And how would I please you, elder?" she asked. She tried to spit her words out with spite, but they came only as a whisper.

"Beg for his life, dryad. You are the only one who would. His mother abandoned him long ago out of shame."

"How will you even find him?" she asked.

"I have found him already. He is with the queen he loves so much. Together, they will stand in mute witness to the return of the world's power to the fae. Tonight, the wizard Thomas activates the spell that will destroy human technology. When it does, the humans will beg for scraps from our tables, and we will laugh as we deny them."

Oriane controlled her emotion, not wanting to spend any of it on tears, but one drop rolled down her cheek to land on her gown and wet it.

"Only one tear from you for your dear boy? And you do not wish to beg for his life?"

"I will beg for nothing. You have no mercy within you. The dryads know that Avenall's mother never abandoned him. You left her to die in the forest of the wounds you dealt her. The dryad's sight is everywhere."

Shan's words roared forth like the cry of a ghoul. "She bore a dragon tender!" He leaned into her cage as he screamed the words out. "She was not worthy of me!"

Oriane's fading whisper answered him back, gentle and yet more forceful than the words he shouted. "Yes, Shan, that is true. No one has ever deserved you."

He shoved the cage, making it swing back and forth on its chain. The motion made her sick. She closed her eyes to fight the nausea. When the swinging stopped and she opened them again, he was gone.

She tried to reach for the crack between the stones, but she was too weak. The effort was too much. Her head slumped to her chest, her body relaxed and pitched to the side.

The guard outside her chamber heard her body fall and

peered through the window of the cell's thick wooden door. Sadness shadowed his face as he left his post to summon the healer.

Thon carried the dryad's body from her cage. The healer had found no life in her, and there was nothing left but to dispose of her remains. It was a shame that such beauty was lost. Although Thon had asked many times over the past days to be allowed to bring her soil, he'd been denied. Elder Shan was a stern leader, and his word was law. He could not disobey.

Even so, he wouldn't burn her as he was instructed. He couldn't. He had more respect for the dryads than his leader did. The dryads had long lived in harmony with the elves. He would return her to the soil as is the way of the forest people. He gently lay her body down in the cart he'd brought to the front of the council house. He covered her and wheeled toward the gates.

With the humans no longer outside the compound, he would have no trouble finding a quiet place outside to return her to nature. In the flames he would later ignite to give the appearance of disposal by fire, he would burn the body of a goat instead of the body of the dryad. The dryad would already be with nature.

Avenall was disoriented at first when he found himself inside the cell in the elven compound, still holding Lizbet's hand. He oriented himself quickly and turned around to the empty cage.

"No, she's not here. It must be the other cell."

With a sprinkle of pixie dust, he and his queen disappeared again to reappear in the identical cell on the other side of the wall.

This time, their appearance did not go undetected. A guard had just opened the door, carrying a bucket of water. When he saw Lizbet, he gaped for a moment then went to one knee on the stone floor. "My queen, forgive me, I did not expect anyone to be in this cell. I have been sent to clean it now that the prisoner is gone."

Lizbet was surprised that an elf would still bend his knee to her. "You may rise," she said, keeping her eyes fixed on him, ready for any sudden move. "Avenall, do you know him?"

Avenall moved forward to stand beside her. "Yes. He's called Thon, and he is a guard here in the council house."

Lizbet addressed the guard again. "We're here looking for a dryad named Oriane. Was she here?"

"She was. But she was kept from the soil too long, and she died. Shan would not allow her even the smallest pot of earth."

Lizbet heard Avenall's sharp intake of breath at the news but knew she couldn't turn to comfort him if she was to continue to appear regal.

"You don't agree with Shan?"

"No, my queen. Not all elves agree with the cruelty of our elders. But we dare not speak up. We have no power against them."

"Then I ask of you that you tell no one we were here."

"As you say. I have not seen you."

Lizbet tossed pixie dust into the air and took Avenall's hand, giving it an extra firm squeeze before she pulled him into the aether.

CHAPTER TWENTY-EIGHT
Warriors

GURRDENN CRAWLED STEALTHILY ALONG the ground next to Eamon, both of them as silent as the dead gnome they'd spent the night mourning. Eamon was surprised the gnome was avoiding flatulence, burping, and other disgusting and attention-attracting gnomish behavior. They stopped where the dense bushes that hid them turned to grass. Gurrdenn made a motion with his head in the direction of a tent in the clearing. Freoric's hiding place. At last.

Eamon began to crawl backwards as silently as he came so they could return to where Hamish and the other gnomes waited. He indicated for Gurrdenn to do the same. Gurrdenn ignored him and leapt to his feet at the edge of the clearing, screaming out a war cry that was no less blood-curdling for being broadcast in the high-pitched tones of a gnome.

Eamon heard the other gnomes crashing through the bushes behind him at Gurrdenn's signal. Their cries alerted the assassin, who watched the gnomes run toward him with amusement. Eamon didn't have time to get out of the way before the other two clambered over him on their way to a useless battle.

He had no choice. He had to join them or it would be the end of them. Just another reminder to never trust a gnome to do what you tell him. He'll disappoint you every time.

Freoric used his knife and his feet. Gurrdenn went down to a well placed kick, but he got back up as the other gnomes attacked, swarming up the elf's legs, trying to reach the tender parts at his abdomen. Freoric slit them and tossed them in quick, practiced movements.

Gurrdenn was stopped by a stomp when he rushed toward the elf again: the loud crunch from his leg when his enemy's boot came down on it should have signaled a stop to his attack. But again, he gained his feet unsteadily, hopping along on his good leg and dragging the bad one, chanting to himself, "Kill elf, kill elf, kill elf." The elf just laughed and pulled his foot back again for a kick that sent the injured gnome flying.

When Freoric saw Eamon coming toward him, he retreated into the woods. Even an assassin thinks twice before entering into a fight with an angry gruagach.

Hamish arrived then, and Eamon yelled to him to tend to the injured gnomes as he bolted into the woods to follow Freoric. He probably couldn't capture him on his own, but he could track him anywhere.

He'd followed only a few hundred yards through the stand of trees before the elf stepped out onto a trail leading toward a cement silo and ran to it, entering it and shoving a rusted steel door closed behind him. The place buzzed with magic, and Eamon would not pursue the assassin into an enclosed area alone. He pulled out his phone and made a call to his queen.

~~*

Following Lizbet's instructions, Eamon hurried toward James's place. She'd told him to meet her there, so he'd shooed Hamish to the silo. He told him to stay put and keep an eye out to make sure Freoric didn't sneak away. Hamish protested, said the gnomes needed him, but he accepted his duty.

Eamon arrived at James's apartment as he was pulling into the driveway after a long night of ghoul-watch in a local cemetery. Eamon couldn't imagine why anyone would face down a ghoul intentionally, but James seemed to take it in stride. Myrddin would have done just the same—if it was a thing that needed doing for the good of others, he would do it without hesitation.

James greeted him with, "Tell me you're just here to bring me a soft pillow and a tasty herbal concoction to help me off to sleep."

"Right. I'll tell you that if you like, but it would be one of those tricksy fae moments that come back to bite ye."

"Yeah, whatever. Do I have time to get a cup of coffee and brush my teeth before you tell me what you've got up your sleeve?" James asked as he started up the stairs to his apartment, motioning for Eamon to follow.

"If you must. But do it while you're devising a plan to restrain Freoric. The gnomes found him but not without a casualty. Hamish and I sat mourning with them overnight for the one of the huddle that ended up buried."

James's face darkened with anger. "I never should have agreed to use them like this. And Bobby's going to be so upset."

"Aye, I hope Trerrfrn wasn't one of his special friends. Gurrdenn's in bad shape, too. Hamish will patch him up as best he can as soon as he can get back to them. All three of them will be out of the spying game for a while. Not that we'll be needing their services if we can catch our prey today."

James splashed cold water on his face at the sink. Then he put a wet hand on the back of his neck to soothe the angry red patch he knew was growing there. "Where's he at?" He took his toothbrush from a cup, wet it, and sprinkled a concoction of herbs across the bristles as he spoke.

"He's holed up in some kind of round cement contraption. The air around it, even from a good distance, fair crackles with magic. Hamish is supposed to be keepin' an eye on him, but I thought it best that no one gets close until we've had a chance to study it thoroughly."

Lizbet materialized in the living room behind Eamon as he spoke. James was surprised to see her there when he turned back to ask another question. "Not only the jester, but the queen. Looks like I'm not getting any shuteye today."

Lizbet crossed the short way across the small apartment and slipped into his arms for a hug before she said, "Yep. Sorry about that. I just dropped Avenall off to grab his dragon. I hated asking him, but he'll meet us there. He's just had a bad shock about a good friend of his. He really shouldn't have to deal with this right now, but I don't want to risk Freoric getting away, and I know he doesn't either."

"How about Tanji?"

"No, she's at the shop with Thomas after school today.

If we get her, he finds out. And I definitely don't want that to happen. We don't know how he's going to react to us going after Freoric."

Eamon interrupted. 'Glad to hear you've got it all sorted. But can we take off now? Because Hamish will do his best to keep an eye out, but I know him, and knowing he's left three injured gnomes behind will keep him from being his most attentive. He'll want to get to them."

~~*

Avenall dismounted and rubbed Fein affectionately behind one ear, communicating to him to follow at a safe distance to keep from frightening the gruagachs. Avenall turned to join the others who were waiting at the edge of the woods. As they started down the path, the dragon went skyward.

Eamon led the way with James. Avenall walked beside his queen. "When we capture Freoric, where will you hold him?"

"I'll take him to the under-castle in Scotland. There are chambers entirely surrounded by rock which can only be accessed by an aurae with the powers of the aether. There are air vents, of course. Aisha will make sure he can't get out and hurt anyone prior to his trial."

"Good. An elven assassin is seldom captured and even less often kept."

"Do you know Freoric?"

"No, I have only heard of him. But what I've heard would give a wise warrior cause to avoid him. He is well known for his skill in both battle and treachery."

"Good of the elves to send him as an ambassador."

"They could as well have sent a banshee. They wish only

to cry death in the face of the humans. I apologize for my race. They have lost their honor, and I am ashamed."

Lizbet reached over and squeezed his hand. Inside her, Morgan stirred to his touch and made Lizbet hold on to her old friend just a moment longer than she would have without her. "It's okay. Eamon says if I respond to them with strength, they'll bow to my position even if they don't want to bow to me."

"Perhaps. But I think the elves will never truly accept a human ruler of the fae. Instead, I see them joining the ungoverned ones—the good folk, the forest gnomes, the sons of Bacchus, and the other wild folk. But I think the elven sense of their own superiority will chafe them if those are the people with whom they must break bread around the table."

"Okay. So, I have no idea who you're talking about— good folk, sons of Bacchus?"

"Do you not? Queen Morgan worked hard to keep the peace with them even though they had no interest in allegiance."

Lizbet was silent for a moment before she decided to tell him the truth. "I don't have her memories. Please don't spread that around, though. I'm okay with most of the fae thinking I do. I'm apparently scarier that way. But I only have the memories of the human Morgan Le Fae. And I don't think she knew anything about any wild folk."

"I am honored by your trust in me. The wild folk agreed as partners to Myrddin's truce. Your James should be able to draw on his memories to advise you. You must be prepared if the wild folk come out of the woods."

Eamon glanced back at them with a scowl and said in a low voice, "If you chatterboxes don't mind, I'd ask you to keep it down a bit. No point in alerting him now that we're nearly there."

Lizbet's eyes narrowed slightly in response, but she didn't ask Avenall any more questions. As usual, Eamon gave good advice despite his bossy tone.

In another hundred feet, they entered the clearing where the wide gray cylinder projected at least eighty feet into the air. When Avenall stopped at the edge of the clearing to wait for Fein, a wisp slid past his knees, continued on to slip between Lizbet and James, floated across the brown winter landscape and straight up the silo wall, disappearing at the top as it dived inside.

James turned around and walked backward as he addressed Avenall. "Looks like we found those wisps."

As they approached the silo, each of them started to hesitate and move more slowly. Eventually, they all stopped walking within paces of each other. Lizbet's heart was racing. She couldn't understand why she felt so frightened. It felt like the freak-outs she got when she was a kid and was afraid to step off her bed because she was sure the monster underneath would grab her ankle if she did. Some nights, she'd lain there awake for hours, afraid to move. She had the same paralysis now.

She broke the silence. "So, anyone else having a desperate urge to turn around and get out of here?"

The two guys and the gruagach nodded their heads, eyes wide as they looked around at each other.

"So, Eamon, you were right about the magic charging the atmosphere here. I say we back up a little to clear our heads."

Lizbet turned and walked purposefully and slowly away, taking the lead on keeping her head even though she felt completely off of it. The others followed her example.

When she reached a distance where her racing heart slowed again to normal and her skin no longer felt charged with electricity, she turned to her followers and said, "Anybody know what's up with that?"

Three heads shook at once.

"Lassie, if the spell's not dangerous and just manipulates emotions, we might try to take a great run through it to the other side before the effects hit. Freoric's inside there, after all. It would have to affect him if he's at the center of it instead of outside of it. But I don't see Hamish here, so he may have come out and Hamish followed him. Despite that, I'm more inclined to believe Hamish just went back to the gnomes to help. He's soft that way." Eamon shook his head, but his eyes were gentle even as he spoke the words of reproach.

"Are you volunteering to see if you can get through that? Because you're not going to catch me walking back into it on purpose. I think we need to figure out if Freoric's still in there or not before anybody does anything."

"Aye, I'm volunteering then, if there's no other way. We can't just let him get away because we're too afraid to try."

"If you get through and Freoric is there, you cannot encounter him alone. I will accompany you," said Avenall.

Lizbet turned to James. "Do you have anything in your bag of tricks that could get us past this?"

"If I had anything, I'd be working on it already. Even Myrddin was smart enough to pass a magically protected area by. He knew better than to mess with anything someone had taken the time and energy to wrap in bad juju. I've got nothing to remove that spell or shield against it."

Avenall turned to her and bowed his head slightly. "It's decided then, if it please you. Your gruagach and I will approach this fortress to see if we can breach it."

"*My* gruagach?" Lizbet laughed out loud, and it felt amazingly good after the gut-squeezing fear of a moment ago. "Avenall, you're a cool guy, but you have no idea how things work in my world!"

Avenall looked confused but Eamon assured him, "Times have changed, laddie. You have a great deal of catching up to do in the area of who gets to tell who what to do. My thought is you'll like it. All right, ready to go?"

"I am."

"Then run like another clan's dragon is in hot pursuit. On the count of three. One, two, three..."

Avenall and Eamon took off running with Avenall trailing behind the swift gruagach he towered over. James took Lizbet's hand as they watched the two runners tearing toward their goal. Within a hundred paces, Eamon began to stumble, pulling hard for breath, and then he collapsed. Avenall continued toward him, scooped up the fallen gruagach, then turned with him in his arms even as he showed signs of failing. His breath came in ragged gasps, and his face was a portrait of expanding terror. He stumbled but continued running steadily away from the cause of his distress. Lizbet started toward them, forgetting the consequences, but stopped and backed up quickly when she was also seized by the dread.

When Avenall reached the edge of the clearing, he went to his knees and gently lay the still unconscious gruagach on the ground.

James picked up his wrist, feeling for a heartbeat, then turned to Lizbet and asked, "Do gruagachs even have a pulse?"

"I don't know. It's never come up." Her face scrunched up with concern.

As James worried about the lack of pulse, Eamon spluttered awake, gruffly pulling his wrist from James's grasp and muttering, "Well, that was a fine plan. What I want to know is who's going to stop me the next time I decide to go waltzing off with the eye of the storm as my dance partner?"

Freoric sat cross-legged with his back to the smooth wall of the silo. He'd watch the queen's collection of warriors through a slit in the door as they'd followed the gruagach up the path, but he had no fear of them. The thing would be done this night, the Abomination had assured him of it, and then Freoric would have his reward. It gave him joy to be so near the end of his assignment.

He closed his eyes and yawned. The gnomes had disturbed an otherwise enjoyable slumber. He had nothing to fear from the children outside and their pet gruagach. A nap would do him good.

CHAPTER TWENTY-NINE

Feet on the Ground

MONA WOKE AND SLOWLY pushed herself up from the bed, still groggy despite the many days of rest, but feeling the powerful pull of the earth. She stood and wobbled, then her hip crashed into the night stand next to Lizbet's bed. She caught herself and stood straight and still until the wooziness went away. She rubbed her side for a moment, contemplating the gigantic bruise she'd have the next day.

It didn't matter. She knew the pull must be a sister dryad reaching out to her. If she was, it had to be important because any dryad who was not already captive risked herself if she communicated to the queen's dryad. She had to find the strength to get outside and plant her feet in the ground.

Sheila appeared at the door just as Mona felt wobbly again. She rushed forward to prop her up. "You shouldn't be up and about. You've been trapped and hurt for weeks. You need to rest."

"I know, but I'm feeling a powerful pull from the earth. I have to connect. I have to. It's Oriane, I know it. I have to find out what she needs to tell me."

"It..." Sheila didn't want to be the one to tell her what her daughter had discovered about Oriane, so she sighed, and said, "It never stops with the fae, does it?" Then she turned her head and called, "Bobby, Mona and I need your help to get her down the stairs."

With Sheila on one side and Bobby doing his best to shore up the other, Mona managed to travel slowly down the stairs one careful step at a time. In the same way, they supported her through the sliding glass doors at the back of the house and crossed the concrete slab that served as a patio, finally ending in the grass.

When she was standing on the open ground, she gathered all her strength and stood straight, digging her toes through the short, well-kept grass into the dirt below. She took a small bottle of potion from her pocket and drank some to deaden the pain of the transformation. "You'll need to stand back now," she said.

Because Bobby was present, she turned her back on her helpers and untied her robe but did not remove it. She had learned to put aside human modesty, but she didn't think Sheila would approve if she exposed her son to his first strip tease.

Mona was able to see them still as her human senses were taken over by her dryad ones. Sheila gently pulled Bobby back toward the patio, where they stood watching the dryad as she changed. He had never seen Mona transform before. His eyes grew wide as she raised her arms and they slowly became branches. He continued to watch with his eyes growing wider still as her roots, small at first, and then increasing until they were thick and strong, grew from her feet and pushed into the lawn. The robe she wore split down the back as two thick branches pushed it out and shredded it against what had become bark from smooth flesh.

It took about fifteen minutes. Bobby was silent the entire time, almost not blinking. When the transformation was complete and Mona's leaves rustled in the breeze, he laid his head against his mother's side and said, "That was freaking cool."

Sheila nodded and squeezed his hand. "Yes, it sure was. Double-freaking cool."

Avenall climbed into the saddle across the dragon's back but didn't pat him with his customary affection as he mounted. His thoughts were elsewhere. The dragon snorted at the slight. He patted the dragon's neck half-heartedly in response. "Take us high, my friend. We do not want to risk being caught in the spell."

The dragon soared into the air. Avenall had to hold tight. The angle of Fein's flight was steep, and he risked falling off if he loosed his grasp with either his hands or his knees. He breathed easier when the dragon leveled out and began to flap slowly toward the sky directly above the silo. Avenall joined his mind with Fein's and guided him to look directly down as they passed over it. Avenall was unsure of what he saw, although he did see the assassin leaning against the wall of the upwards tunnel. Yet in the center, there was something that he did not understand.

He instructed Fein to circle around and fly over again. This time, the dragon's eyes picked up more detail and he realized he was looking at a round, glass container filled with the shifting shapes of wisps. Why someone be collecting wisps? Why would anyone, human or fae, have anything to do with the soulless things? Even dragons did not intentionally go near them.

Having seen what he could see, he directed the dragon back to where the others waited for his report. He didn't know what it meant, but he would tell it as best he could.

～～*

Avenall hunkered down and used a stick to draw what he had seen during his flight in the dirt at Lizbet's feet. His voice sounded lifeless, disinterested. His eyes were dull, all of the light gone out of them that had been there before he'd heard of Oriane's death. "Freoric is there. He may be resting. He may be laying in wait. I do not know. And here, in the very center, is a globe of colorless glass within which can be seen the moving outlines of wisps. The globe is dense with them. Someone must be gathering them for a purpose."

"Freoric?" Lizbet asked.

"No. Freoric does not have magic to do what I've seen."

Lizbet nodded. "You're right. It has to be Thomas. I guess I still want him to be innocent for the first time in his lives, even if it's only for Tanji's sake."

Avenall's eyes sparked a little when he heard Tanji's name. "I'm sorry for Tanji. I know what it is not to fully understand what is in the heart of another." For a moment he paused, eyes closed tight and averted as he thought of Oriane, then continued, "But I fear for her as well. And I would not wish for anything to harm her. She's promised to teach me to dance."

Lizbet smirked. She couldn't help herself. "Oh, I bet

she has. And I don't want to see anything happen to her, either. But it's going to get dark soon, and I can't think of anything else we can accomplish here, so we might as well go home. Eamon, can you keep an eye on Freoric tonight to make sure that he doesn't decide to take off?"

"Aye, glad to, mistress. I'd ask, however, that you locate Hamish and the gnomes. I'm concerned they haven't turned up yet." Eamon stepped to James and handed him a handkerchief. Or, at least, something that might once have been a handkerchief. "I borrowed that from Hamish back in the old world many years ago. You should be able to use it to locate him, as he's never stopped ownin' it despite having stopped havin' it."

As James took the dirty rag gingerly, Lizbet's phone rang. She listened intently, asked a question or two, and then said, "Really? That's amazing! Avenall will be so happy. And yes, thank Mona for me." After she hung up, she said, "Change of plan. Whatever Thomas is doing, he's doing it tonight. We need to get Tanji away from him right away, even if we can't stop whatever he's going to be doing... and Avenall," she said, turning to him, "Oriane is alive. Apparently you don't want to bury a dryad without making absolutely sure she's dead."

She could see moisture forming in the corner of his eye, but he brushed it away with his forearm and smiled broadly, relief washing over his handsome face.

"So...Eamon, you stay here to make sure Freoric stays put. James, I'd still like you to find the gnomes since you'll be able to help them if they're hurt."

James's mouth quirked into a half smile. "Sure, let Eamon have all the fun."

"Yep. And Avenall, you're with me. We'll also be needing that dragon of yours. This is my best friend we're talking about. We need the big guns. Do you think he'll pitch a hissy if he has to carry two?"

She could see Avenall considering the question and coming up blank.

"I mean, will he be okay with that?"

"Yes, he will carry two comfortably."

"Cool. If not, I'll pop off and fly behind. But I've kind of been looking for an excuse to ask for a ride, and now I've got one."

"Yes, Tanji enjoyed it. I am sure you will, too. I understand that it is, what did she name it? 'Totally bitchin'.'"

CHAPTER THIRTY
Girl In A Cage

L IZBET HOPED NO ONE would object to her parking a
dragon outside Magic On Main. As she approached,
she could see Thomas behind the counter, lit up by
the lights inside. He was idle, keeping his eye on a couple
of customers who were looking at the shop's selection of
rune jewelry.

He greeted her cheerfully in a self-important tone when
she entered the shop. "Queen Lizbet, what brings you to
Magic On Main today?"

At this, the customers at the jewelry counter turned
and looked at her. She didn't know them. Probably from
out of town. One of them nudged the other toward her.
She so completely didn't have time for the celebrity thing
today. She looked directly at the nudger, focusing her magic
in the irises of her eyes, where it glowed as a fierce, blue,
intimidating fire. It made her vision blur when she pulled

that trick, but it looked darn impressive. It was apparently more than the tourists had counted on when they met the fae queen for the first time. One of them bobbed her head nervously in greeting, then they turned and left the shop at a faster pace than tourists normally managed.

"Way to chase off the customers," Tanji said as she entered from the back room. "'Cause like, who needs those, right?"

"Whatever. I need to talk to you, Tanj. Let's go to the coffee shop or something."

"Right now? We're closing shop in a few minutes and then Thomas is taking me out for dinner."

"No, I had this thing happen today. I need to talk to you, really. You'll probably need to spend the night. It's one of those kinds of things."

Thomas broke in then, pointing to the street. "Why is that elf here? Isn't he the one who betrayed his compound by stealing away with the dragons?"

"Yeah, that's the guy—he's just dropping me off. And you don't need to worry about why my subjects turn up here. You can leave that to me."

"As you say, my queen. Forgive me." Thomas said, sounding less than sincere. "It's just that Tanji and I have a special dinner to go to. I need her more than you do tonight."

"Look, Thomas, it's girl stuff. You wouldn't get it."

Tanji grabbed his hand where it sat on the counter and squeezed it. "Yeah, sweetie, we can do dinner tomorrow. We can even hang out all day if you want. We could try some ice-skating. You've never been, right? And you said it looked interesting when we watched the kids at the outdoor rink a couple of weeks ago. The rink's open all afternoon on Saturdays."

"No. It has to be tonight. I've got something for you

after supper. It's more important than 'girl stuff'. You can't keep casting aside our relationship every time your mate stubs her toe and wants a natter."

Tanji had to look away. She fought to keep from laughing when he accused her of being the one who hadn't been putting time into the relationship.

Lizbet's temper rose. "Look Thomas, I don't want to have to command you to do it some other night, but as your queen, I could do that. So stop pushing."

"Maybe I no longer want to follow a human queen. When the fae discover you have nothing of queen Morgan inside you, they won't follow you anymore, either."

Before Lizbet had time to think about his complete 180 change of opinion, Thomas sprang over the counter and grabbed Tanji by the hands, dragging her toward the back room.

"Let me go," Tanji shouted, struggling against his grip. She tried to dig in, but her three inch heels gained little traction on the glossy faux-stone floor of the shop.

Lizbet raised her hands to cast a ward and trap Thomas before he could get her out of the room, but he sent a blast of percussive energy toward her that knocked her painfully on her behind before she could complete the spell. She caught herself on her elbows before her head went back against the hard floor.

She winced with the pain, and when she opened her eyes, she watched Thomas pull his hand down across Tanji's face. Tanji immediately slumped in sleep. He bent over and slung her over his shoulder, then straightened and ran out through the back as Avenall entered from the front.

He knelt down to her, his face overflowing with concern. "What did he do to you? I'll will find him and bring him to his knees."

Lizbet rubbed a sore elbow. "Yeah, that's a great idea right about now, but he has Tanj. We need to track them but make sure she doesn't get hurt when we try to rescue her. I still don't think he'd hurt her no matter what he'd do to me, but I'm not going to take a chance on us being the ones who put her in pain."

They hurried to the waiting dragon, leaving the shop unattended. She was climbing into the saddle when she realized she'd left the shop unlocked. Tanji would kill her when she found out. She rushed back, locking the front and rear doors with magic because she didn't have the key. That should keep her friend from ripping her head off later. Because there was no doubt in her mind that she'd soon have Tanji back.

James rubbed his palms together to end the locator spell that had led him to the gnomes. He really hadn't needed it once he got close. The usual noises that accompanied gnome activity were enough once he was in range.

It was clear Hamish had done the best he could with the injured. He'd attended their wounds, tearing his own clothing to provide the bandages, and he sat next to the two pale gnomes laid out on the ground beside him with a glum expression on his face. Gurrdenn's leg was in a splint and the bandage around his head was stained with blood. However, his expression was still fierce and full of fight as he nodded in greeting. James felt sure that Gurrdenn was going to be fine.

"I'm sorry, I couldn't leave the wee things alone in this state. And I couldn't carry all of them with me. They're small, but so am I. And I might just have hurt them worse if I'd tried."

"Hamish, you did good. Don't beat yourself up about it."

"I might have wished for a better conversationalist than this one, though," he said, cocking one thumb toward the gnome chief. "Not really one for chitchat."

Gurrdenn grimaced in response.

"Yeah, well, that leg doesn't look good. I doubt he's up to entertaining anyone right now. But it's going to have to wait for a while longer. From the look of things, these other guys are in more danger." He turned to Hamish. "I need you to get into my apartment and bring me the black bag I've got stowed in the closet. It's got a red cross on it in a white circle. Can you do that for me?"

"Aye, I can. I'll be back with it in two shakes."

Hamish ran off with the surprising speed of the gruagach. James could hear him breaking through the brush with little concern for the branches that lashed him as he went. Gruagachs have tough hides, much like gnomes. But neither of them have hides tough enough to fend off a magically-enhanced elven blade.

He wished Tanji was here to help. Tanji was a better healer than he was. She was quicker to diagnose, and the people she healed recovered from the effects of her magic faster. What she and Thomas accomplished for Mona had been miraculous. Even so, he hadn't liked Lizbet going off with Avenall to get her, even if the elf did have a dragon to call on. He would have liked to have been the one to be there for her if things got dicey.

He was also still having a hard time accepting that his friend and former roommate wasn't who he seemed to be. Thomas had loosened up a lot when he first started dating Tanji. How could you not become more fun with her around? But then he closed up again and returned to a twenty-four hour a day focus on magic and magical society. Plus, his bromantic interest in Freoric was nothing short of pathetic. It had surprised everyone when Freoric stopped avoiding him. He should have seen what was going on. He might have stopped it.

As James assessed the gnome's wounds, he felt anger building inside again and knew he'd have to focus it in a positive way if he was going to do them any good. He was sure that Freoric had taken advantage of Thomas and led him astray. And there's no way a few gnomes could have been a real threat: Freoric didn't have to hurt them like this.

He sat cross-legged next to the gnomes and ran his hands over their bodies, feeling slowly along their abdomens and limbs, using his anger to fuel his magic, feeling for the aura of blackness that indicated the site of an injury. The first gnome's wound was easy to find. He was bleeding freely from his side, and Hamish's bandage had only slowed the flow to a trickle. But it was the only wound, and although it went deep, it didn't seem to have pierced any of the unfamiliar organs James could sense in the gnome's small body.

The second gnome had fared much worse. In addition to the external wounds, James sensed a spreading blackness in the gnome's abdominal cavity that could only mean his systems were shutting down. If Hamish didn't get there soon...

And then the black bag was there at his right hand. Hamish had made a several mile round trip in mere minutes. *Note to self—get a gruagach*, thought James. *These guys are handy.*

He quickly removed the herbs he needed and mixed them in a small bowl with some of his own spit, then applied it as a poultice to the worst wounded of the gnomes. He had Hamish hold the gnome's mouth open as he poured in a few teaspoonsful of the contents of a blue glass bottle. It stunk, but it should stop the spreading blackness in the gnome's abdomen. The gnome spluttered as the liquid hit the back of his throat. James hoped some of it had gotten down to where it could do some good.

Finally, he extended his hands face down over the gnome's small body, and a pale blue glow jumped from his palms to bathe the gnome's belly in light. After a moment, the glow stopped and James removed his hands. The gnome looked better, less pale. He burped once, with more gusto than he'd managed before the healing session. It was time to move to the next.

He finished faster with the second gnome. The little guy revived immediately under James's care. Hamish had to shush him and threaten him sternly with additional harm if he didn't just lay still.

Finally, he turned to Gurrdenn. "Are you hurting anywhere that I can't see, Gurrdenn?," he asked.

"No. Leg. Head."

"Good. Then I think I can help."

The head wound was superficial and healed quickly, leaving only an abraded patch of skin after a few minutes under the poultice. His leg was more difficult—Freoric had broken it in several places. James was amazed the sharp edges of bone hadn't broken through the skin. So, yeah, it could have been a lot worse. As he applied the magic to knit the bones back together, Gurrdenn's expression softened from fierce to grateful. When James was done, the gnome stood tentatively on his damaged leg, then put his full weight on it, and began to walk toward the silo.

"Good," he said in his limited English. "Good wizard. Now, we kill elf. Come."

"Not a good idea, guy. You do know you're limping and wincing, right? You've got to give that leg some time to finish healing."

"We kill elf. Come."

James looked at Hamish, hoping the gruagach had some suggestion for how to handle the determined gnome, but Hamish only said, "Nothin' more bloody-minded than a gnome when he's set himself to it. You may just want to follow him and get it over with."

Having no other plan, and knowing that he'd done the best he could for the other gnomes and was now leaving them in good hands, he took a few minutes to build a protection spell around Hamish and his charges. Then, he fell in behind Gurrdenn on his slow tramp through the woods.

Thomas's magical strength was not the only power increased by his absorption of the wisps. His physical strength had also risen, and he had no trouble running with his girlfriend's weight across his shoulder. He took a direct route through the city and then the woods, clearing any obstacle in his path with a wave of his hand and a blast of magic. He'd planned it out so carefully: the dinner, the flowers, the spell, and then they would be on their way to the French compound where they could practice magic among their own kind with no more interference from humans.

It would have been so romantic, so right, and Tanji would have loved it. She'd always hinted to him of her need for romance. And Lizbet had spoiled it for them! But Tanji wouldn't forgive him if he punished her for ruining the special evening he'd planned. And he very much cared what Tanji thought. He'd done all of this as much for her as for himself.

When he reached the clearing near the silo, Eamon turned when he heard Thomas coming down the trail and ran toward him, shouting, "Thomas! What are you doin' with that poor lassie? Put her down!"

Thomas blew the interfering gruagach off his feet and into the tree line with a wave of his hand.

On the other side of the clearing, James came into view behind the small, slow-moving figure of a gnome.

"I don't want to hurt anyone, James. But don't interfere with me tonight or you'll find out the hard way how powerful I've become."

James wasn't afraid of Thomas, but he couldn't risk a lightning pulse or other attack without potentially harming Tanji. He watched Thomas hurry into the silo and close the metal door behind him. It clicked shut and then disappeared, leaving only a solid concrete wall where the door had been.

Tanji woke within a magical bubble. Thomas stood with his back to her, chanting with his arms high in the air. She put one hand onto the light blue barrier that surrounded her, and it went through. She stood up and started to walk out of the bubble but was overcome by dread when she did. She gasped aloud at the force with which the terror hit her and shrunk back against the wall, safely encapsulated again. Her terror abated.

Thomas turned to her, and his face was kind. "I'm sorry I had to take you the way I did. But you need to stay inside that boundary until it's time for us to go. It protects you from the spell."

"You may think you're protecting me, but all you've done is put me in a cage. Let me out. I know you don't want to hurt me."

He went to her and took her hands in his. "I would never hurt you. All of this is for you. When it's done we can be with our own kind and be free to practice magic without human interference. We'll be with family. People who are like us, who care about us. Who don't laugh at your ears or fear your gift."

"Whatevs. I *am* with people who care about me, and I'm fine with things the way they are, even when people don't get me. People have never gotten me. So you can let me out now. This is not a good date night!"

She continued to try to sway him, but he tired quickly of her arguments. He cupped the side of her face gently with one hand. "I know you'll understand in time. But I have to get back to work now."

He motioned to Freoric, who brought him a small case full of the components of his spell.

"The table..." He waved his hand in the direction of a small folding table and Freoric carried it to him, set it up, then stepped back out of the way. Thomas laid out his herbs and tinctures, taking a pinch of this and a drop of that, adding each to the globe that swirled with the essence of the wisps.

He chanted as he worked, sometimes in the Elvish he'd learned from Freoric, sometimes in English, sometimes in the old tongue he'd learned from Myrddin through James. Tanji wasn't able to catch all of the words because a mouthless scream was building slowly within the globe, making it hard to hear him. She knew his words were potent because the air was charged with power. The essence of the wisps glowed brighter and brighter, becoming painful to watch. She felt sure that Thomas was glowing, too, now, as he pushed himself forward in an ever greater use of his magical power.

It grew too bright, and Tanji couldn't watch the scene playing out before her any longer. Even that evil freak Freoric seemed affected. He'd withdrawn as far from the globe as the round walls of the enclosure would allow, shielding his eyes with one hand. She covered her eyes with her hands and put the tips of her thumbs tight into her ears in a useless attempt to drown out the scream that filled her world.

CHAPTER THIRTY-ONE

Boy Falls From The Sky

JAMES RAN TO WHERE Eamon stood waiting, composed again after his unexpected flight into the bushes. Gurrdenn limped repeatedly toward the silo and then limped away again with a little more speed, not learning as quickly as the others that the spell was coming from the silo and couldn't be breached with bravery alone. Fein touched down at the edge of the clearing and Lizbet slid off his back, then Avenall urged him skyward again.

Lizbet ran to James, hugging him. "Are you okay? We saw what happened from up there. Avenall's going to take a closer look at what's happening inside that thing. And then we're gonna need a plan."

Avenall made several passes, mentally mapping the location of people and things within. Tanji looked so small and lost as she leaned against the side of the silo. His resolve to use his newly discovered power one final time grew. He didn't feel good about it. It wasn't something he wanted to do. But if he could force Thomas to peacefully stop what he was doing, it could prevent people from being hurt. He hoped he could use his power without the others knowing what he'd done. He didn't want to have to run from this new home like he had his old one.

He communicated to Fein that he wanted him to hold steady above the silo. He hoped he would not feel the same blank space he'd encountered when reaching for Freoric's mind. No, Thomas's was there in sharp relief, buzzing with magic. He sent a pulse of thought telling him to stop what he was doing, leave the silo, then lay down on the ground and go to sleep.

As the command arrived at its target, he felt it stop and reflect back to him. Thomas looked up, smiling, as Avenall stood and surfed the dragon's back, then made the motion of opening a door and stepped off into the sky.

That he was falling rapidly toward the ground barely registered. He felt so sleepy.

He regained control of himself when Fein flew swiftly to catch him and carry him in his claws to the ground. The dragon did his best not to cause harm, but a claw dug into his shoulder just enough to hurt and disrupt the command he'd ended up sending to himself. It was much less than he deserved for continuing to use a power he knew was taboo. It didn't matter if no one else would know what he'd done. He knew what he'd done. It was past time to tell the truth.

When he returned to the ground, he went down on one knee to his queen and bowed his head low.

"I said don't do that anymore. And what happened up there?"

Avenall kept his head bowed. "My queen, I am ashamed. I've used a forbidden power, and I've lied to a friend about it to protect myself. I beg your forgiveness and ask that you allow me to help you with Thomas before you decide my fate." He raised his head briefly to look at James. "I'm sorry I did not tell the truth when you asked me. I was afraid."

James nodded. "You shouldn't have been afraid. I just wanted to be sure about what I'd seen. I wasn't judging you. Mostly, I just wanted to know whether or not Lizbet was safe with you."

"Although I can probably guess what you're talking about, you want to fill me in?" Lizbet said.

Avenall explained. "The power of the dragon tender to enter the mind of others is no myth. I discovered this before I left my compound. I used my magic to communicate with a dryad who was imprisoned there. Then, when a dragon rider discovered my preparations for escape, I pushed a thought to him to go to the weapons room and go to sleep. I also used the power to prevent a man from getting too close to the dragons while I was traveling on the ship. I made him turn and walk away. What you just saw happened when I tried to push Thomas. He was able to push the magic back at me."

"So basically what you're saying is, you used your power to talk to someone who was in trouble, to make someone else take a nap so you could try to prevent a war, and then forced someone else to walk away from a dangerous situation. Right?"

"It sounds different when you say it, but yes. That is what I did."

"And this is a problem because...?"

"This power is wrong. It takes away a person's own will."

"Yeah, well—if you do it for the wrong reasons and in ways that harm people, we'll have a chat. But we all have magical abilities that can be used in the wrong way against other people's wills. I'll let you know if I see you doing something evil, okay? I agree you probably want to keep it under your hat, though."

"My hat? It is not..."

"Not tell people about it, I mean," Lizbet interrupted him.

"As you say." Avenall relaxed visibly and stood again. "I had hoped I could stop this conflict today if I used my power, but there still must be a way for me to enter the silo. If Freoric and Tanji are in there, the spell must not affect people who are inside. I could drop from Fein's back. If Thomas pushes me back up, Fein can catch me. It would have to be from a safe distance so Fein is not himself affected, but I feel sure I could do it."

"Correct me if I'm wrong, but elves aren't much tougher than humans when it comes to smashing themselves up, are they? You'd never survive a jump like that."

Eamon seconded her. "Aye, you wouldn't, laddie. But it's not a wasted idea. I'd have no problem with a fall like that. It's the sort of a jump I do for a spot of fun. My only concern would be fallin' on the lassie and causing her harm."

"I've got my bag of tricks. I'm pretty sure I could whip something up to help with that," said James. "That explosive thing I do—I could package up a small one for you that would push you away from the walls if you're going to land on anything you don't want to land on."

"Right then. As usual, several heads are better than one."

While Avenall described the layout inside the silo, James worked quickly, then handed Eamon a packet of powder wrapped loosely in paper. "Just toss it and say the magic word, which is this." James held up a piece of paper on which he'd scribbled the word BANG. "And no wisecracks. I'm wingin' it here. It'll blow you in the other direction when it goes off. It won't be much of an explosion, so it won't knock you out if you hit the wall."

"Or an assassin, with a bit of luck."

Avenall headed toward the dragon and Eamon followed, accepting a hand up to the dragon's broad back. Gurrdenn trailed after him and started to climb up, too.

"Go on, get off with ye. We're in a hurry."

"Kill elf. Come."

"Might as well take him," said Lizbet. "Wasn't it you who told me how tough gnomes are?"

Eamon grumbled but stretched a hand down for the gnome to grab and helped him clamber up behind.

Avenall checked that they were all hanging on tightly to their little piece of the saddle and then gave the dragon leave to enter the sky.

* ~ * ~ *

Avenall called back to the gruagach seated behind him. "You'll only have one chance at this, small one. I'll make several passes so that you can choose where to land carefully."

"Oi! Who're you callin' small one? And you do know I'm hundreds of years older than you, right? You best be addressing the gnome, laddie, or you and I'll be having a parley after all this is done."

"I apologize. I meant no offense."

"I'll let it pass this time." Eamon leaned out as far as he could over the dragon's side to look down into the silo below him. "Och, not a lot of room in there, is there? Not a lot of places to land."

Gurrdenn piped up behind him. "Kill elf." His hand rested on the hilt of his small, sheathed knife.

"Right you are. I expect you're all ready to go then, are ye?" Eamon asked, looking behind him.

The gnome grinned and nodded.

"I'll try for Thomas on the next pass. I'd try for the globe, but I have no idea what the consequences might be of knocking it over. I'd ask where you plan to land, but I think I've guessed your target. I'll go on the first pass, then you follow me down when the dragon doubles back."

Gurrdenn, who'd lowered himself by climbing down Avenall's long leg while Eamon gave him his instructions, looked down and saw Freoric beneath him. He didn't wait his turn. His chilling scream as he fell might have been a war cry.

"Och, I hate gnomes! Get us over the top again quick as you can!"

Avenall urged the dragon into a tight turn, and Eamon bailed out after patiently watching for his target to appear. He was all intensity now, prepared for a battle. He hoped it was one he could win.

He neared his target, but the gnome's arrival had alerted the wizard below. His movement stopped in midair when Thomas caught him in a magical tractor beam emanating from the top of his upstretched hand. For a moment, Eamon felt the dread again. It was overpowering. He also felt the first scream of terror in his entire long life welling up inside him. Then Thomas brought his hand down, depositing him into the bubble with Tanji, who grabbed him and hugged him close. At least he wasn't going to scream. He disentangled himself quickly from Tanji's protective arms.

She said, "Don't go back outside the bubble. We're only safe in here. I don't know how Gurrdenn can stand it."

Eamon had forgotten about the gnome in his fright but looked across to the other side of the silo where the gnome clung to the elf's shoulder, biting into it. He lifted his head up once to take a breath and spit out a small piece of flesh. His face registered terror, but he didn't stop until the elf finally got a good grip on him and held him out at arm's length to have a look.

Freoric laughed then. "I am impressed. You would make a fine assassin with training. I may even let you live."

The sputtering gnome continued to kick and grab for him even as he dangled helplessly in the air. "Perhaps I'll keep you for a pet. You do amuse me."

Eamon held Tanji back as she instinctively started toward the gnome. "Lassie, there's nothing we can do for him. Help me think—whatever Thomas is doing, we've got to stop it."

"I don't know what he's doing. But I think he's almost done with it. You can tell he barely even knows anyone else is here now."

Eamon turned his attention to Thomas's face and saw that Tanji was right—he looked transfixed. You could see the magic flowing across his skin as he chanted and moved his hands across the globe that contained the shifting, living swirls of magic formed by the concentrated essence of the wisps. The surface of the globe began to roil. Peaks of magical energy exploded up toward the sky and then abated. Thomas chanted louder and louder, but his words were unintelligible. It was a language older than even the old tongue, and Eamon didn't know it. Thomas shouldn't have known it, either.

Eamon knew if Thomas had tapped the ancient magics, there would be nothing they could do to stop him.

He tried to dash across the room to the globe, but he only got two steps along before he shriveled into himself in fear and had to turn back.

When he'd recovered, he hung his head into his hands

as he said, "It's no good. There's not a single thing I can think of. All we can do is watch."

~~*

Thomas had been barely aware of his surroundings when he lowered the gruagach into the bubble to be with Tanji. He was acting on pure instinct now, the magic having taken control of his actions. His instinct knew that Tanji would not be happy with him if he harmed these insignificant lower fae she called friends. It was this instinct alone that saved their lives. Thomas was busy elsewhere.

Within the swirling shapes in the globe, he saw the fae's salvation. Human technology and weaponry—the guns and bombs that projected death at a distance—would be suppressed for all time. The lights of the cities would be extinguished, the vehicles would no longer outpace horses, the phones would all stop ringing. Only the forms of weapons that existed in the time before the life of the shadow realm would function. It was the next step in the evolution of the world, a world that had been ruled for too long by humans. And what had their rule brought? Cities of concrete and steel that sprawled out to destroy what once had been endless forest. Nature was the true source of power—the ancients knew it and respected it. Most of the humans had forgotten. But humans would be reminded. It was what he'd tried to explain to Tanji, but she just kept telling him that he needed to stop what he was doing because no one would understand why he did it. No one would forgive him.

But he knew they would. They would be happy when they again found their way.

He was one with the magic now as it exploded upward.

His heart sang with it: he was power, he was light, he was the magic itself. He had never felt so alive.

He urged the swirling essence of the wisps to enter the sky and create the new earth they would guard: the lost spirits of magic would be his soldiers in the sky, forever vigilant and self-sustaining.

He raised his head and his arms. He called up to the sky and the stream of magic followed his voice into the air, finally bursting above the top of the silo in a thin column and reaching up to the clouds where it began to disperse. It shaped itself at first in a mushroom cloud but soon thinned at the edges and transformed from glowing cloud to glowing mist. It spread quickly in all directions, dampening the light of the stars and rushing toward the horizon.

Thomas watched, and there was nothing in all the world that could disturb him.

Freoric tired of the gnome's antics, annoyed that while the gnome was slowing down, it hadn't yet succumbed to the spell fully and given in to unconsciousness. He flicked it across the room just as the column flared. It didn't stop kicking and yelling gnomish obscenities even when it disappeared into the column and shot skyward, caught in the updraft.

When the blue column burst from the silo, Fein panicked, bolting backward in flight in a way Avenall hadn't known dragons could do. The bucking motion nearly cost him his mount for the second time that day, but he managed to hang on to the pommel and climb back to his seat when the dragon regained his composure. He turned his gaze to the column. It was the blue color of magic with the same swirling shapes as he'd seen inside the globe. And then, he saw something else, something more solid.

It was...by Bacchus's whiskers! It was a gnome.

He didn't stop to think what danger the column might present. He urged the dragon toward it, instructing him to fly close but not to touch it. He didn't know what would happen when he came in contact with it, but his mind was focused only on saving the gnome who had been his companion for so brief a time.

As the dragon sped along the column, following the upward path of the shadowed shape of the gnome, Avenall held tight to the saddle with one hand and reached out into the bright beam of magic with the other. It stung like a thousand bees, but he didn't pull back until he had the gnome's leg firmly in his grasp. When he did, the gnome hung there lifeless.

Avenall turned the dragon toward where the others waited, hoping James had just a little more healing magic left.

CHAPTER THIRTY-TWO

Darkening Sky

L IZBET HELD HER BREATH as she watched Avenall lean out toward the column and reach in to save the gnome. When he grabbed the upward hurtling body and pulled it from the column, she exhaled sharply with relief.

The relief was real, but small: they hadn't stopped Thomas. Whatever this column meant, whatever this film spreading across the sky like an oil spill was going to do, it was going to happen.

She moved closer to James, who held her tight. They could do nothing but watch as the stars dulled.

Avenall brought the dragon down, leapt off quickly, and lay the silent gnome out on the ground for James to examine.

James moved his hands over the gnome and said, "I think he's fine. No bleeding, no dark spots in there. Looks like the magic just knocked him out. He doesn't have any injuries."

"Good," Lizbet said. "Good..." She looked to Avenall, "...and Tanji? And Eamon?"

"I'm sorry, my queen, I don't know."

She stood, waiting. It was all there was to do.

It wasn't enough.

As she waited, the glow of city lights that hung above the tops of the trees on the horizon disappeared. It was suddenly so dark where the column of magical light didn't reach.

It felt like days but was only hours before the globe was empty and the sky full. Thomas lowered his hands but his skin still glowed faintly with his power. He turned to Tanji and said. "We'll be going soon. The journey won't be long. Freoric has a ship waiting for us. A proper sailing ship with a strong crew. We'll be in France before you know it."

"I don't want to go to France. This is my home. I just want you to undo whatever you did and go away. Far away. I don't want anything to do with you."

Freoric interrupted. "You can quarrel later. I demand proof now that this spell has done what you promised."

"And you've got it. Right next to you. Pick up the torch. You know it was working an hour ago when you used it to rummage through your pack."

Freoric flipped the switch on the flashlight and nothing happened. "Yes, as you say, this light shone an hour ago. And this—this was a functional weapon when I took it from its owner," he continued, reaching into a deep pocket and pulling out a pistol. "I know because he didn't like that I took it. I had to test it on him. Let us see if it is working now."

Thomas didn't flinch as the hammer clicked down on the bullet. Nor was he surprised when nothing happened. "And now you have your proof. Let's go. Help me with these things." Thomas looked at the wall where the door had been, and the door appeared again. Then he turned to gather a duffle-bag and pack he'd previously stowed in the silo. "You'll need to run interference if Tanji's friends try to stop her leaving with me. We'll all make up someday, I'm sure, but for now I want them kept away without being harmed."

As Thomas spoke, he was at first surprised, then angry that the elf grabbed him from behind, his arm tightening around his body. Thomas's voice flowed low and dangerous when he said, "Are you thick as well as disobedient? Don't you remember what I just did?" Thomas flicked a hand, and a burst of magic meant to immobilize Freoric passed through the elf with no effect.

Freoric pulled him even closer and then Thomas felt the sharp edge of the elf's long hunting knife under his ribcage. "And don't you remember you made a ward to prevent me from being affected by magic?"

The blade bit deep as Freoric thrust the point upward toward Thomas's heart. Thomas slumped downward. He looked up into the elves' eyes and asked, "Why?" as he slid downward.

Freoric leaned down to whisper in his prey's ear as his life flowed away, "Why? The Abomination asks me why. But you have always known I was an assassin."

Laughing, Freoric stood and used one foot to shove

Thomas's body face down into the dirt. Then he wiped his knife clean on Thomas's back before sheathing it again.

* ~ * ~ *

The gnome woke up when the silo door opened to discharge Freoric with his pack and bow slung across his back. Freoric glanced at the humans, then walked purposefully and unhurriedly into the woods, his back to them. Gurrdenn bounded up and wobbled toward him on unsteady legs, still intent on revenging his friend and huddle-mate.

"Gurrdenn, stop!" Lizbet called, but the gnome had already wandered far into the spelled zone. Still, he seemed to be gaining speed, not losing it. She turned to James, "Do you think..."

"Only one way to find out." They both tore toward the silo with Avenall behind them.

When they reached the door, Lizbet looked cautiously around the doorframe and his eyes met Tanji's where she sat on the ground, Thomas's head on her lap, and her hands covered with blood. Eamon stood next to her with a hand resting on her shoulder.

Tanji said, "He wasn't all bad. He could have killed all of us, but he didn't," as the tears streamed down her cheeks. "You know that James, he wasn't all bad..."

She reached for James's hand behind her, and they walked into the silo together.

Avenall spoke from the doorway after they'd gone inside to Tanji. "I'll locate Freoric. You must stay and comfort your friend." He left with the gnome trailing behind him. After Avenall mounted, he waited for Gurrdenn and stretched down a hand to boost him up. He would not refuse the company of a proven warrior on this search.

They flew low across the forest in the direction Freoric had gone.

James tried to start his car, but like all of their technology, it was dead. They left the useless vehicle and walked toward town and the police station. Thomas was a human. His body was not the responsibility of the fae, and they would have to report his death. It was probably also a good idea to let the authorities know the electricity wouldn't be coming back on any time soon.

Lizbet's supply of pixie dust was played out, so she couldn't carry them all through the aether. No one said anything about it, but she could feel none of the others wanted to be alone either. The four friends walked along the side of the road together as Tanji told them the full extent of what Thomas's spell had done.

The night was so dark without the glow of the streetlights or passing cars. There was no one on the streets. Lizbet figured most people would just assume it was a power outage like any other and go to bed early. Except in the morning, there would still be no power, and everything about their lives would be changed.

With no flight paths over town, no planes would have fallen out of the sky here. But there would have been accidents as cars stalled and electrically assisted brakes suddenly needed an enormous push to work. Closer to the lake, planes would have come down with no way to land them safely. There would be ships stranded at sea with no way home. Hospitals with no source of power. Thomas might not have been all bad, but because of what he'd done, whether he was all bad or not didn't make a difference.

"What do you think the media will call this one since Fae Day's already taken?" Tanji asked, still sniffling but trying to put on a brave face and not completely lose it.

"What media?" replied Eamon. "They'd have to go house to house like town criers, ringing their little bells."

"The Faepocalypse?" said Lizbet, shrugging. Her voice sounded lost, defeated. "Trendy and catchy."

James threw his arm around her shoulder and gave her a hug. "Yeah, that's my queen." He pulled out his phone and said, "Anybody want to listen to some music?"

"Sure, that'll work...oh wait, it won't." Lizbet took out her own dead phone and said, "Might as well not even carry this around anymore, right?"

James took it from her and said, "Except we're fae. Sort of. We have a power source." As he held the phone in his hand, it started to glow and then the screen lit up, displaying the time and the lock screen.

"Sure, as long as you keep feeding it magic."

"No...I don't think we have to. I just filled it up, stored some like you'd store it in a battery. Like..."

He set it on the ground, took his hand away from it, and it stayed lit. "I set it up so that it will run for a while, losing just a tiny bit of magic as it goes. You know how starweed, some of the other herbs, and lots of magical creatures can absorb magic? That even includes some humans who can fiddle around with low levels of the stuff. Why can't we figure out something that does that—pulls the magic out of the atmosphere and feeds it back to power what electricity used to power? I mean, like on a big scale. A really big scale. I mean, isn't that what Thomas's globe was doing? This could work until we can figure how to undo whatever he's done."

"I cannae believe there's really that much free magic floating about."

"Sure, sure there is—what do you think the Tree of Life used to keep the shadow realm going? Magical creatures pull their magic from somewhere. It's not like they're just born with what they're going to have, and if they use it up, it's gone. It's more about the size and shape of the reservoir. When Thomas filled me with wisps, he increased the amount of magic I could carry as a human from almost none to a lot. And when I use it, it isn't just gone. It takes a while to recuperate, but I get it back. It's all around us. Every day. I just didn't think about it before because who needed to? That's something Thomas would have thought about..." James went silent for a moment as his throat suddenly tightened, making it difficult to speak normally. He took a deep breath to relax it and went on when he'd recovered. "He was the philosopher. I'm practical. But now that it's practical to think about it, I can see how some of this can be put right."

Lizbet turned and said, "Your car! Let's try your car."

The group hustled back to James's car, and he magiced up the battery. The lights turned on, the radio played white noise as loud as they liked, but the car still wouldn't start. James closed the hood and leaned on it heavily. "That should have worked. I put enough magic in there to power twelve cars. He did something else besides just turning off the electricity. Scratch the idea of just a 1:1 replacement of magic with gasoline. I bet it has to do with combustion. But the battery is working. I bet an all-electric car would run."

James looked around, then walked swiftly to a telephone pole at the end of the road where a transformer hung grey and dark next to the electrical lines. He looked intently up at the transformer, then turned his palms toward it. A bright ball of magic slowly lifted up to the metal container, then buzzed slightly as it pushed up through the bottom of the housing. When it did, the streetlight closest to the transformer came on.

Then, the streetlights slowly began to light up one after another. When the magic reached the row of houses, the lights within started to light, too. "See? The magic can flow just like electricity, although it'll stop after a while instead of just spreading out forever. But it will flow along the lines for a couple of miles, I think. It may last a week or two, and then it will need to be renewed.

Lizbet threw herself into his arms. "You know you really are kind of amazing, right?"

"Sure. I know." James grinned.

"Can you teach me to do it?"

"I think so. I can probably teach any fae to do it. It's just about hooking into the magic the right way. I can probably even teach the gnomes to do it. Think how popular they'd be then! Who's going to complain about the state of their garden when they're keeping the lights on for you? Tanji's father would be making a living transporting gnomes *to* people's houses instead of away from them."

Lizbet wrinkled her brow and her tongue worked around in her mouth as the ideas started to flow. "Gnomes, huh?"

CHAPTER THIRTY-THREE
Something You Forgot

THE NEXT EVENING, TANJI sat in the cold in the Moore's back yard with the porch light off even though James had powered the house and she could have turned it on. Her eyes were red and hurt when she was in the light. Avenall stood solemnly beside her.

He asked her, "Were they awful, these human policemen? Are they like elven law dealers? If they are, then I hope you do not have to go to them again."

"No, they're not awful. But just...just leaving him there at the silo and sending strangers to take him..."

"I would have brought him here for you, if you'd asked."

"He would have liked that. Being cared for by his friends before burial. He prepared the body of the fae queen Morgan in the old way when she died after being separated from Lizbet. But Thomas was one hundred percent human. His magic came from wisps, and it's not the human way

239

anymore—at least not in middle class America—to be prepared for death by your friends. I don't think I could bear it. Even if I wanted to, I don't think I could live as fae."

"And even though I am elf, I will no longer be allowed to live as one. Elves are communal. It's not our way to be alone, yet I am outcast. But then..." He stopped, pensive. "...it has been so long since I felt I had any family among the elves."

Tanji took his hand, just being friendly. Nothing flirty. The very thought that she might be flirting made her remember the first few times she'd talked to Thomas, and he'd blushed at her innuendo even though he was way older than she was. And that made her want to cry again. "Look in there—do you see those people?"

Avenall turned to look at the scene in the house. Around the table, Mona, Sheila, Steve, and her own father played a game of cards—the game was often solemn, but they were there for each other all the same. Bobby stood behind his mother, then ran behind Ron to peek at his cards, and a big grin broke out on his face. James sat on the couch with Lizbet, her head on his shoulder, listening to music on his phone.

When Avenall turned back to her, she said, "Those people, those amazing people, are determined to have just one last normal evening before the Faepocalypse really hits and everybody realizes that this is not going away. Most of them aren't related to me, but those people are my family, my community. And I'm pretty sure they'd be happy to be yours, too. Because this community is going to need all the help it can get."

"I recognize your father. Is your mother among them?"

Tanji's dark skin turned pale. "Ohmigod, my mom. I spent so much time feeling sorry for myself that I forgot about her! She left for New York yesterday. She's going to be in the city without electricity. It's going to be bad there! I have to..."

Tanji bolted off the picnic table and ran for the house, pushing the sliding glass door too hard, so that it made a jarring sound when it hit the end of the track.

"Lizbet, you have to take me to New York. Moms will be alone there!"

Lizbet looked up and immediately understood. "We'll bring her back here right now. Come on." She poured pixie dust into her hand from a pouch she wore on her belt. "James, will you come, too? New York might be a little scary right now."

It only took a minute before Lizbet tossed the pixie dust and the trio disappeared.

It was dark in the Manhattan apartment. Tanji spread some starweed from the collection of powders and potions she kept in her purse and quickly lit the room. She walked to the bedroom, then to the bathroom and kitchen. It was a small apartment and easy to search. Her mother wasn't there.

Tanji began to tear up. "She left yesterday, so where could she be?"

"Maybe she got caught on the freeway when it all went down." Lizbet offered her hand again. "Look, we'll go back and we'll do a locator spell. Right? It'll be okay."

The three friends disappeared again to the aether.

James completed the spell and bound it to the blank sheet

of typing paper Lizbet supplied. Nothing. No blue glow to indicate Mrs. Ross's location.

"She's out of range of the spell, Tanj. I'm sorry. But there are stronger spells I can try. Just let me go over to my place and grab my notebooks."

Tanji sat quietly with her father's arm around her while James ducked out to get his books. She tried to stop her tears, but they kept flowing just the same. When James returned, he sat at the table and paged through the notebooks quickly. He made a noise every so often. Sometimes it was an optimistic sound. Other times it was a discouraged one.

"Okay, here's the good news. We have most of the ingredients of one of these spells available, and it has a really long range—like, if she's anywhere in the United States, it'll lead you to her. The bad news is that the main magic is either a narwhal horn or a dragon claw."

Tanji snuck a look at Avenall, but she said nothing and just as quickly looked away. His face clouded, then he made a decision and said, "I can supply a dragon claw."

Between slow breaths to try to keep herself from sobbing, Tanji said, "You said that's all you have of your friend now. You can't."

"Yes, but this claw is not my lost friend no matter the emotion I attach to it. It is only a reminder. I won't forget my friend if I give this claw so that you can be reunited with your mother. I give it gladly." He took the thong holding the claw from around his neck and handed it to James. "It is my gift to Tanji."

He turned away afterward, to stand looking out at the dark yard through the sliding glass doors.

Tanji started toward him. When she realized his breathing was sharp and shallow, she stopped and just said quietly,

"Thank you, Avenall. Thank you." She turned. If he didn't want to be seen crying, she wasn't going to push.

Avenall kept his eye on the locator spell James had bound to his hand while he simultaneously rode in the minds of both the dragons as they flew. When he glanced to his side, Tanji was holding tight to the pommel on Harul's saddle. She didn't display the excitement she'd shown on her first ride above the barn. Now, she tensed against the cold, her face empty of expression.

The blue dot which had taken two hours of flying to creep toward the center of his hand began to increase in size. Avenall guided the dragons downward. When they landed on a darkened freeway, Tanji scrambled off Harul quickly and ran to Avenall to look at the map on his palm. She darted into the darkness in the direction the dot indicated. Avenall hurried after her and found her at a vehicle, looking in the windows.

"This is her car, but she's not in there."

As she spoke, the blue glow on Avenall's hand winked out. Tanji looked into his eyes with fear.

"No, this is good. The disappearance of the spell means that we've found her." Avenall had to believe this. He'd given up the last thing that bound him to his loved ones. He could not have that be for nothing. He knew his heart would always feel emptier without Durian's claw resting above it.

"Tanji?" The sound came from behind the car.

"Mom?" Tanji ran around the car and into her mother's arms, where her mother was walking up a small embankment. "We found you!"

"Toonkins, how did you get here? How did you even know I was here?"

"I'll explain it when we get home. I hope you don't mind getting there on a dragon."

It was well past midnight when Lizbet hugged her friend good night after delivering the Ross family home through the aether.

When she returned quickly to her family room, her mother was already helping Mona up the stairs, but Avenall stood stiffly near the sliding door, watching Fein doze in a growing pool of melted snow in the backyard. James was cleaning up from both the magic he'd cooked up earlier and the dishes they'd used for dinner.

"Avenall, you're welcome to stay the night. Bobby would love to have a real live elf crashing in his room. But he'd probably keep you up all night with questions."

"No. I thank you, but I merely wished to tell you good night and wish you a good trip when you travel to meet with your elders."

"Yeah, it'll be an interesting one, that's for sure. Except I hope I'll be seeing you again before then. We're going to be needing help from just about everyone when we get back, so please come for the meeting tomorrow afternoon. It's not just about getting the lights back on in town. We've got to get a system in place to get them going quickly for everyone everywhere. We're going to need a lot of gnomes. I think they're going to become popular little guys pretty quick."

James snapped his fingers and pointed in Avenall's direction. "Oh, by the way, I forgot to give you this back, Avie."

He walked across the room and handed Avenall his dragon claw. Avenall looked down at it, confused.

"I thought you needed it for your spell. Did you not need to use it?"

"I mean, yeah, I used it. And it was kind of a mess to get cleaned up again—it had a lot of gunk from the locator potion stuck to it—but I think it cleaned up okay. Not quite as good as new, but close."

"I thought..."

"Sorry guy, I didn't tell you you'd probably get it back because I wasn't sure. In fact, I'm kind of surprised it made it through. If there'd been any flaws in it, it would have broken and dispersed in the spell, but it held up great. I won't ask you for it again. Its usefulness for spell-casting is played out, but it should hang together for you just fine as jewelry."

Lizbet watched Avenall's expression change from somber to beaming. He looked like he wanted to say something, but the words didn't come.

Then Lizbet remembered what she'd meant to tell him before he left. She was so tired from the events of the evening that she was a little woozy and wasn't firing on all pistons. She was never going to make it through all of her responsibilities for the next few days if she didn't work in enough sleep.

"Avie, you and I need to take a quick trip tomorrow morning. Mona communicated with Oriane again while you and Tanji were gone. She asked that I take you to her as soon as possible. She has something for you."

"It cannot be anything as nice as having Durian's gift returned to me, but I will go with you gladly. I miss Oriane. It will cheer me to see her."

"Cool. We'll go before the meeting."

CHAPTER THIRTY-THREE
It's Always Darkest Before The Dawn

IZBET LET LOOSE AVENALL'S hand as they appeared just outside the Elven compound in France. She turned when she heard a whisper say, "This way—quickly! The guards have been more active outside the compound since the change in the skies and will soon walk their rounds."

They followed swiftly behind Oriane as she entered the forest. When she stopped and turned in a small clearing, she took Avenall's hands and said, "I have missed you, my dear Avie. But I am glad you are now somewhere where you are treated the way that you deserve. Mona tells me you are among friends."

"I am. I have many friends now—Tanji, Gurrdenn, James, and the queen's family. There is little else I would wish for other than to have you closer to where I am."

She reached her hands up to gently frame his face with

her hands. "Oh Avie, I cannot be near you. This forest is my home. But there is something I have longed for years to give you, and now I can. You must protect it with your life. Can you, Avie? Can you promise this?"

"I would deny you nothing."

"Good, then close your eyes."

Avie did as he was told. Oriane dropped his hands, and he could hear her moving away, her soft step rustling the forest loam. Then the rustle returned to him, and she took his hands again. It confused him when her voice came from several feet away saying, "Now, open your eyes."

He opened his eyes and was immediately blinded by his own tears. He held his mother's hands, not Oriane's. She looked older, with scars on her face and arms, but it was his mother just the same. They wrapped their arms around each other and she pulled his head to her shoulder to comfort him as she had when he was a child.

"How are you here?" He stood back from her with his arms on her shoulders, looking directly into the loving eyes he remembered so well.

"The dryads found me and healed me after your father left me in the woods to die. I could not let you know because your father might have found out. I've waited all this time, hungry for every word of you brought by Oriane. But now, if you will take me to this other land where there are no elves..."

Lizbet took that as her cue. "Have pixie dust, will travel..." She raised a hand above her head to sprinkle the dust she'd pinched from her pouch.

"Wait. Please..." A male voice sounded from the edge of the clearing. Avenall recognized it and looked toward the source. It *was* him, Durian, coming out of the woods.

They went to each other and grasped each other in

a hug—more affection than elven men should show to another, but Avenall didn't care.

Durian stepped back but left his arms on Avenall's shoulders. "It is good to see you," he said. "I have missed you since that day I ran away and left you on your own. Oriane asked me here, but I've been so ashamed, and I did not want to burden you. And yet here I am, and I do not want to live a solitary life anymore. If I could, I would also go with you."

Avenall looked toward Lizbet, questioning.

"Hey, the more the merrier. Right?"

He thought he was seeing things induced by the strain of trying to read by candlelight when the red-headed girl and her companion materialized in the middle of the Presidential Seal that covered floor of his office.

The armed men posted inside the office door sprang immediately to alert. The tall young man in front of him raised his hand casually in their direction as they sprang into action toward the twosome. Instantly, the guards stopped moving, paralyzed in place.

"Sorry," said the young man, "I figured this would be kind of a beat-up-first-ask-questions-later scenario for you guys. Needed to get in the first shot, so to speak. They'll be fine in a minute. Just as long as they don't take another run at us. I'm pretty quick on the draw."

The girl waved at him in a friendly way. "Hi. My name is Elizabeth Moore. You may have heard of me. I'm Queen of the Fae. And this is James. He's my muscle." The corners of her mouth turned up in a private joke when she thought of slim James being anyone's "muscle". She was still tired and a little giddy from lack of sleep. "We're here to help with the power problem. We could take care of it on our own, but we need to know the best places to start—hospitals, water distribution plants, farms, places where they package food. And you'll need to help us set up distribution that doesn't depend on machines. I'm thinking lots of horses. Maybe bicycles pulling trailers. Whatever works."

She took a breath and smiled charmingly. "So, we'll get all that straightened out for you, although we don't think there's anything we can do about the phones and the walkie-talkies and the internet. It looks like any form of modern communication just isn't going to work. And really, don't even think about asking for help with the weapons. Just don't. But the rest of it—although we've already celebrated Thanksgiving, I think most people around the world will have something to give thanks for again by the first of the year if you're willing to work with us."

The President stood, nodded, and motioned them to sit. "I'm listening."

"Okay, so here's the first step," said James, as Lizbet moved to take the chair that was offered. "People are really going to start appreciating gnomes..."

ABOUT THE AUTHOR

Jill Nojack is a writer, musician and artist. She has published several short works (stories and poetry) in small press. Her first published novel, Magic Unbound, Book One in the Fae Unbound Series, was released in November, 2013.

When she isn't exploring her creative side, Jill enjoys laughing too loud and long in public, long bike rides, and talking about herself in third person. She resides in the great American Midwest with a long-suffering cat and makes her living as a computer tech, because, if you're lucky, that's what you do with degrees in English and Sociology.

Visit www.faeunbound.com for more information about the series along with related special content. You can sign up for the newsletter if you would like to be notified of sales, new releases, contests, and special content for newsletter subscribers.